Rising over Darkness

A story set during the Russian invasion of Ukraine

Matthew Ashworth

ISBN: 9798355839505

Contents

Introduction from the Author

Thank you for picking up this book.

In this book I wanted to show and explore the struggles ordinary Ukrainian people have been going through during this invasion. It follows entirely fictional characters but during real events that occurred in the first five weeks of Russia's full-scale invasion of Ukraine, starting at 24th of February 2022 and ending at the start of April when Russian Federation forces retreated from the north and north-east of the country after a failed attempt at besieging the city of Kyiv. The focus of the events here is not on intricate military strategy of the battles or the political events that occurred, but rather the focus is on the personal journeys of ordinary people. The fictional characters in this book go through the experiences that many ordinary Ukrainians went through.

I would like to apologise in advance that some scenes in this book are emotionally very heavy and will be challenging to read. However, atrocities such as those described in this book did occur in reality and affected thousands of peaceful civilians in Ukraine, and I wanted to represent this unjust and barbaric invasion with as much accuracy as possible.

I would also like to mention that all the royalties earned from sales of this book will be donated to helping Ukraine through the UNITED24 organisation. The reason why I chose UNITED24 is because money donated through it goes directly to helping Ukraine and doesn't get held up with any middle men. I highly recommend to make donations to Ukraine through UNITED24.

This book is dedicated to all the brave and wonderful people in Ukraine and everyone supporting their effort to stay free and independent, people such as the soldiers fighting on the front line, doctors and nurses working hard to save as many lives as possible, firefighters and rescue personnel, other civil servants keeping the country running in a crisis, people who have lost loved ones because of this war, people who have lost their homes, people who have been forced to flee their home, people who have lost their jobs and sources of income, people who have been injured or crippled as a result of shelling, people who have died as a result of shelling, people whose mental state hit rock bottom, people whose education has been negatively impacted, and also not to forget, the brave people who have rallied against the war at the protests in Russia in the early days and risked getting arrested for it. May there be peace in Ukraine soon. Slava Ukraini!

Map of Ukraine

Here is the map of Ukraine with all the city and town names that are mentioned in the story, as well as a few larger cities that were not mentioned and the neighbouring countries for reference.

Please note that you might've seen many of these city and town names spelled differently on occasions. This is because their names are slightly different in Ukrainian compared to their Russian/Soviet name. For example, Mykolaiv is Nikolaev if Soviet version of the name is used, and Kyiv (Ukrainian version) used to be Kiev (Soviet version). In this book, I used only the Ukrainian version of each city name.

Chapter 1

24th of February
Mykolaiv

In a sharp shock Solomiya woke up to the blaring and dreadful sound of
the air raid alarm. Her head was spinning and she was utterly confused,
unable to comprehend what was happening. She felt her throat convulsing
and her heart racing in her chest. As her senses came to her and she
regained awareness of her surroundings, she understood what this
horrifying sound meant – it meant the worst had come. The war had
started and there was no going back.

Mere seconds later she heard booming noises in the distance and planes
flying by very fast. *"Explosions already?"* was the first question in her head.
She jumped off her bed as quickly as possible and rushed to the window.
Tymur, her partner, was also up by now.

"Don't stand so close to the windows, dear. It's dangerous," he said as
soon as he saw where Solomiya was standing.

She listened to his advice and stepped away from it. More explosions
were heard in the distance, each one causing her to shudder in fear.

"We need to get to safety. They're bombing us already," she spoke in a
slightly trembling voice, still coming to terms with the situation.

With great haste the two of them put on their coats right on top of the
pyjamas they were wearing and rushed to the front door. They lived on a
third floor of an apartment building and needed to get all the way down to
the basement level where they could take shelter. The other people living
in the same building were also coming down the stairs, running to take
shelter in a sense of panic. Everything felt hazy and unreal, like it was all a
bad dream.

Once on the ground level, they opened the heavily worn down cellar
door and headed down the steps. It was dark and excessively dusty in

there. The air was cold and stale and made Solomiya cough it out the moment she stepped inside. The steps leading down into the basement were irregular and parts of them were chipped. It was very easy to misplace one's foot and fall down, so Solomiya tried to be extra careful and watch where she was going.

The steps ended and led out into a small, square-shaped chamber with dull grey walls, a low ceiling and a mixture of dirt and sand all over the floor. The air was even more stale down there, but nobody cared about that anymore. The most important thing was to get to safety in case the building was hit by a missile. Nobody wanted to die, and staying safe was paramount.

Tymur flicked the light switch in the basement. A couple of small light bulbs went on, giving just enough light to let everyone see the room and the people next to them. Some of the people that came down with them brought flashlights too for some extra light.

"Now I guess we sit and wait," Tymur turned to Solomiya.

There was nowhere to sit in the basement – no chairs or benches, no large rocks or bricks even. Just the unhealthy-looking dirt all over the entire floor. A couple of the people that came down brought blankets with them and set them down on the ground. Solomiya and Tymur, however, did not bring anything to sit on, so they just grabbed an old wooden plank that was leaning against a wall and set it down on the ground.

Once they sat down, Tymur put his arm around Solomiya and pulled her closer to himself. Solomiya rested her head on his shoulder and closed her eyes, feeling scared and trying hard to hold back the tears. The other people also sat quietly and with a pensive expression on their faces. Some were on their phones while others were talking to each other in a low tone of voice. The sudden attack shocked everyone and nobody could fully believe that it was really happening.

Two minutes went by when Solomiya's mobile phone rang. She opened her eyes the moment it rang and took it out of her coat pocket. Her parents were calling her.

"Didn't realise the signal could reach all the way down here," she muttered and picked up the phone. Her father Sergiy was on the line.

"Hi, dad."

"Solomiya, dear, are you ok? Are they bombing your city as well?"

"Yeah," she gave a short reply as she couldn't gather enough energy to explain what was going on.

"And are you still at home?"

"We're in the basement with Tymur and the others. What about you and mum?"

"Kyiv is getting shelled too, so we're also staying in a shelter. Your mum is really scared. Everyone here is. I'm worried for you too. Please don't go outside," Sergiy's voice was sadder now.

"But I have to go to work, dad. I am needed, especially at a time like this."

"I understand. Just… please try to be as careful as possible and only go out if necessary. And keep us informed if everything is fine with you."

"I will, dad. Thanks. You too, please stay safe there."

The call ended here. Solomiya put the phone back in her coat pocket and rested her head on Tymur's shoulder again. Her parents were far away from her, in Kyiv, so she could not physically help them and they could not do the same for her. What to expect from the day ahead was unclear. The more she thought about it, the more it worried her. Her worst fears had materialised – the dreaded war that many were anticipating had actually started and nobody managed to prevent it.

24th of February
Kyiv

The air raid alarm seemed to have stopped for the time being. The 25-year old Oleksiy got up on his feet and walked over to the window in the next room. His mother, Irina, and his sister, Diana, who was only three years younger than him, were also there in the same room. They were in a much more anxious state than he was.

"Is it safe?" Irina asked.

"I don't know. Probably," Oleksiy wasn't sure, but continued looking out of the window to check how things were outside.

They lived in a small apartment block, consisting of only five floors. Their apartment was on the second floor, so they were in a safer position than the people who lived above them. However, upon hearing the air raid alarm for the first time this morning, they all hid in the kitchen, as it was further away from the outside wall than all the other rooms in their apartment. The alarm had a terrifying sound, one they did not expect they would have to hear, but alas this morning it came on, signalling that the war had started and their country was under attack.

Irina and Diana were still reluctant to exit the kitchen, fearing the worst. Oleksiy continued looking out of the window for any signs of the enemy planes.

"I think it's safe for now."

"I still cannot believe it's happening," Diana murmured in a sad voice. "What do they want from us? We've done them no harm."

"It would be best for you two to evacuate from the city," Oleksiy stated after a few seconds of thought.

"Oleksiy, you are also coming with us," his mother Irina insisted.

"It's no point, mum. I won't be allowed to leave the country anyway."

"Then we'll stay here too."

"It's a bad idea. You know that you need to get Diana out of here, out of danger."

"I've already lost your father 8 years ago. I cannot lose you too, Oleksiy," Irina began crying, tears streaming down her face.

"I'll be fine. Dmytro is here. He'll always be around to help me if I need it."

Dmytro was Oleksiy's friend for the past three years and worked in the same car garage shop. They were about the same age and often helped one another. Oleksiy knew he could always rely on his best friend in any difficult situation.

Irina buried her face in her hands, thinking in silence. Diana sat still next to her, taking deep breaths and feeling unsure about this whole situation.

"You'll have to leave Kyiv today," Oleksiy said after a minute. "Russians will likely reach us by tomorrow. Our time is short. You've already packed the suitcases, yes?"

"Most things, yes," Diana confirmed.

"Then we shouldn't lose much time."

It took nearly a full hour for Irina and Diana to agree that it was best for them to flee Kyiv. Oleksiy promised to them that if things got really bad in the city, he would leave it and head to the western Ukraine, where it would likely be safer. He helped them both to finish packing their suitcases and by lunch time they were on their way.

They used the metro to get to the Vokzalna station, which was located right next to the main overground railway station. Oleksiy carried their suitcases the entire way while they walked behind him, shaken and without hope. There were many other people at the station too, also fleeing Kyiv with only one suitcase-worth of possessions, leaving their home behind into uncertainty. Many were with little kids, trying to get the young away from where they could get harmed.

On the platform the crowds were even larger. People were so numerous and so densely packed on the platform that it was a challenge to pass through them even in single file. The atmosphere there was one of fear and sorrow. People were crying, saying goodbyes to loved ones, trembling and holding their kids tightly by the hand. It was a dreadful feeling as though the world was ending.

To Oleksiy the scene of the hectic crowds at the train station platform reminded of the old photos of World War II he'd seen. A feeling of disbelief overcame him within a sudden moment. He felt unusually dizzy and began asking himself if all this was real, and if the events of 2014 that occurred in Donbas were repeating themselves but this time in the whole country. Memories flooded him of the time when he, his mother and his sister were fleeing Donbas when the fighting there had only started in 2014. His father stayed behind to fight, and a few weeks later he was reported among the dead. It was the darkest patch of Oleksiy's life and he never forgot it.

They spent such a long time pushing through the crowds on the platform and queuing up to board the train, that it felt like an eternity. Oleksiy could not tell if only minutes passed or hours. Once they reached the train, Oleksiy handed the suitcases to Irina and Diana. They were both in tears.

"It's not too late to come with us, dear," Irina said to her son.

"I have to stay here, mum. I am of more help here than in the west of Ukraine."

"I understand. Your father would've been so proud of you if he was still alive."

"I know. Please go safely. We'll keep in contact at all times. Let me know when you reach Lviv."

Irina gave her son a hug, not wanting to let him go. Once she released him, Diana hugged Oleksiy too.

"If you are in any danger, Oleksiy, you let us know, ok?" Diana told him after they finished hugging. "Don't go being a hero. Mum and I need you to be alive."

Oleksiy nodded in agreement and watched as his mother and sister boarded the train. It was difficult to be separated from them after having lived all his life with them, but he knew it was for the best, he knew it was for their safety. And perhaps soon in the future they'd be back again or he'd leave Kyiv and be together with them again. Despite the overwhelming feeling of sorrow, he felt a small but noticeable glimmer of hope.

They looked out of one of the windows in the train and met his gaze just as the train began departing. As the train was moving, the sight of his mother and sister in the window was moving further and further away from him too until he could no longer see them.

Once the train was gone, Oleksiy felt an overpowering sense of loneliness and vulnerability. That was it. His dear family was no longer with him and he was all alone in a city that was about to get besieged by a ruthless enemy. It all dawned on him at once and he wished he would've gone together with his mum and sister.

"No, I'm not all alone. I have Dmytro and other friends here. We'll stick together," he convinced himself.

He decided it was a good idea to meet up with Dmytro in the city centre, so from the Vokzalna station he took the metro to the Khreshchatyk station, which was located on the central street of the same name in Kyiv.

Many people were taking shelter in the metro, and the Khreshchatyk station was full of people finding a little corner for themselves and their children. Because it was very cold, most of them wore coats or warm jackets, as well as woolly hats and even mittens at times. Some were wrapped up in warm blankets and had food and some of their possessions with them. They didn't know how long they would be there for and came prepared.

There were masses of people stretching out along the hallways and even on the stairs, everyone scared and unsure of what to expect next. Small children were a little less aware of the situation and were running around and playing with each other, trying their best to entertain themselves. Some of the people had their dogs or cats with them, keeping them company in this difficult time.

Oleksiy was walking past all the people, looking at them and feeling the pain of each one. Many were tired and were trying to get some sleep or were simply at a loss and trying to stay alive.

He ascended via the escalators, reached the surface and headed to where his friend Dmytro agreed to meet him. The air raid alarm continued sounding and many people in the street were in a hurry, either to take shelter or to leave the city. Khreshchatyk and other streets in the centre no longer felt the same as before. There were fewer people around as most were scared to be outside or had already left the city in the days prior. There was a general feeling of gloom enveloping the city and seeping into each person.

Dmytro was already waiting for him at their agreed meeting spot. He was slightly taller and bigger than Oleksiy, and unlike Oleksiy, he had a short beard which was always scruffy.

"Good to see you, brother," Dmytro greeted his good friend. "Air raid alarm did not scare you out of your wits?"

"It's scary alright. But since when did that stop us?" Oleksiy replied and then changed the topic. "Did Vadym say anything about us coming to work today?"

Vadym was their boss who owned the car garage shop where they worked. They had a lot of respect for the man as they knew how hard he worked to get his business off the ground and continuing to operate despite the pandemic and other troubles of recent years.

"He said not to come today or tomorrow as things are quite unpredictable," Dmytro answered whilst gazing all around the street they were on. "None of us knows what hell is going to go down here in the next few days. It's all a mess, brother. I'm not too worried for myself but for Liliya."

Liliya was Dmytro's wife whom he knew since high school and married a couple of years back.

"Does she insist on staying here in the city?" Oleksiy asked.

"Yeah. Says she has nowhere else to go and no-one else to be with."

"We'll pull through this one way or another. We have to."

"Damn right we will. Have you heard, they'll be handing out guns to anyone who wants to fight and defend the city. I think we should each get one too. When those damned Russian orcs come here, there will be a lot of fighting in the city. I intend to be armed and dangerous when they dare to show themselves."

"I haven't thought of that, but it sounds like a good idea. I am not going to sit here in fear and do nothing either. We all need to fight as it seems. What choice do we have?" Oleksiy agreed with his friend. "Do you know where they're going to give out the guns?"

"No, but we'll find out. Let's go."

24th of February
Mariupol

The 17-year old Danyil and his 13-year old sister Lera were both sitting on the sofa and watching their parents who were hastily walking around the apartment and preparing a small bag of supplies. The shelling had stopped temporarily, so they needed to get prepared before it resumed again. Danyil was feeling anxious about his parents going to fight the invaders and he could see that his sister was worried for them even more.

Both of his parents had been serving in the military for several years, and now they were heading perhaps into the biggest fight of their entire lives.

"I wish mum and dad didn't have to go to fight," Lera began, snapping Danyil from his thoughts. "I wish nobody had to fight. Why can't we all just live in peace?"

"I share your view, little sis," Danyil responded. "Unfortunately this world is full of very nasty people, so there will always be fighting."

"One day all this fighting will be the end of us all. Humanity won't survive it."

Danyil gave those last words a thought. He could feel the sadness and hopelessness in his sister and he was feeling really sorry that she had to face this situation so early in her life. And yet there was some truth in her words. He understood perfectly well that constant wars did nothing other than destroy, and in time they could be the end of all humanity.

Their mother and father finished preparing everything a few minutes later. Danyil and Lera got up and went downstairs together with them to say their goodbyes.

"Danyil, we leave you in charge," their mother Svitlana said as she gave them both a hug. "Please take care of your sister, and take care of yourself too. Try to stay out of danger. This may be only temporary, but for as long as the danger persists, please stay safe."

"We will try our best to be fine. We're more worried about you and dad," Danyil said. "You are the ones going into the lion's den."

"Yes, but it's what we have to do. Someone has to defend our beautiful city and the people in it."

Their father Oleg also came up to them at this moment and hugged both Lera and Danyil at the same time.

"Listen, if things get really tough here in the city in our absence, Danyil, you take your sister and get out of here. It will always be dangerous out there while invaders are attacking us, but if it gets worse here, you know what to do," he gave his children his advice.

After giving their children one more hug, both Oleg and Svitlana got in a car and drove away, heading to the front line where they would be engaging the enemy head on. Danyil and Lera continued standing motionlessly and watching as their parents' car departed and disappeared off into the distance. Lera began crying and gave her brother a tight hug, her face burrowing into his jacket. With her parents away and with no certainty of when they would be back, her brother was all she had left at that instant in time.

Danyil was feeling really anxious. The thoughts at the back of his mind kept telling him that this was the last time he'd seen his parents. He tried his best to push those thoughts away, but a part of him found it hard to deny that they might be true. The cloudy grey sky above was only reflecting the same mood back at him and only confirming his worries.

"Sis, why don't you go back inside? I need to go and see Dasha really quickly and then I'll be back," Danyil said after a few seconds flew by.

Lera looked him in the face without a word and nodded in understanding. Danyil waited till his sister went back into the building and then headed to see Dasha. Dasha was his girlfriend who lived nearby and was the same age as him. Danyil knew that she and her family were planning to leave the city if the war started, so he wanted to be sure to see her before that.

When Danyil got there, Dasha and her parents were outside, loading bags into the boot of their car. Dasha saw him approaching, but her face did not light up with a smile as it usually did when she saw him. She looked like a completely different person.

"Dasha, how are you holding up? You decided to leave after all?" Danyil began.

"It's terrible, Danyil. Really terrible," she replied.

"I know. Both of my parents have just left to go fighting on the front line. I don't know what will happen to them now."

"This city is not going to hold for long. You and Lera need to leave it. Why don't you come with us?"

Danyil was at a loss for words. It was unthinkable to just get up and leave the city. And go where? They had no place to go to, no relatives anywhere else in Ukraine or outside it.

"Dasha, I…" he tried choosing his words carefully, "I don't think we can leave. Besides, the road out of here is very dangerous. Every metre of it is within enemy's firing range."

"It's even more dangerous to stay here," Dasha argued. "We either take our chances with the road or we stay here and wait for the end to come."

"I'm sorry, Dasha. I cannot go with you."

Dasha brought her gaze down onto the ground with a disappointment. A tear came down her face a moment later and her lips folded slightly.

"That's it then? We'll never see each other again?" she said in a quiet voice.

"I don't know, Dasha. I wish I could tell you with certainty, but I really don't know what is going to happen in the next few days and weeks."

She took a few deep breaths, trying to find her words. Her eyes were watering even more now.

"I guess it's a goodbye then."

Danyil walked closer to her and grabbed her in a tight hug. She began crying and sniffling quietly so that her parents wouldn't hear her. Danyil did not want to let her go. He wanted her to stay with him so that they could spend their days together and perhaps marry in the future, but the circumstances made this impossible. Dasha was leaving and was likely never returning. Neither of them knew if they'd still be alive tomorrow. They had no clue and no control of where life would take them. There was no point clinging to the empty hope that they might be together again. No matter what they wanted, destiny had other plans and they were powerless to do anything about it.

25th of February
Bucha

It was past midday on the 25th of February already. The shelling in areas surrounding Kyiv was intensifying. A lot more missiles were whistling through the air and more fighter jets were flying overhead. Maria was in the basement of her house, holding her 8-year old daughter Alina close to herself and refusing to let her go. Her husband Artur was also there with them. They spent a few hours that day in the basement, hiding from danger coming from above. The nightmare that started the day before was continuing, and with each passing moment, the reality of it all was infiltrating Maria's mind and terrifying her.

"I think the bombing has stopped for now," Artur proclaimed after some time and opened the door to the outside.

Maria and Alina came closer as well and peered outside. It was calm. Hesitantly all three of them exited the basement and walked over to the front door of their house. A few of their neighbours were also already outside. To their relief no houses nearby were hit by missiles, at least not yet. They lived in a nice and picturesque neighbourhood. Each house was pleasant-looking from the outside and had a small garden.

Once inside, Alina ran to her room, while Maria and Artur sat down in the living room, thinking about how they would get through this. They were still a relatively young couple and had a big portion of their lives ahead of them. And with their daughter growing up, they knew they had to give her the best life possible.

"Surely they won't hurt us, right?" Maria began. "I mean we're just civilians. We mean anyone no harm. And they are like brothers to us. They've always lived among us and we among them."

"If that was so, they wouldn't be attacking us right now," Artur pointed out.

"They probably just want to change the government. That seems to be their main goal. I bet our politicians have fled already."

"Not really. Zelensky is staying in the capital. So is the mayor of Kyiv. And all the others are too."

"Do those guys have a death wish or something? The Russian forces will practically be parading in Kyiv by tomorrow."

"I don't know, dear," Artur gave up. "We just need to worry about staying safe and keeping Alina out of harm's way. That is my number one priority right now."

Maria nodded in agreement and began thinking whilst looking down. She remembered how a couple of her friends were panicking about the possibility of the war starting, but she refused to believe them. It seemed incomprehensible and absurd that Russia would attack them in a full-scale war. And yet it happened anyway, despite how hard it was to believe. If only she listened to her friends and fled the country in time, her daughter would've been in safety now. But then her husband would've been all by himself as men were not allowed to leave the country at this time. She didn't know if staying there was for the best or if leaving was. There didn't seem to be an ideal scenario. The next few days would clear everything up, she thought.

At this moment Alina came up to her mother. She saw how sad Maria looked and gave her a hug. Maria was so lost in thought that she didn't notice her daughter come close to her until the moment Alina hugged her. And once they were hugging, the tight knots of pain Maria was feeling inside began to slowly disappear. She was hoping this moment would never end.

25th of February
Kyiv

Evening time had come in Kyiv. There was a lot more shelling this past day and more plane fighting could be heard in the skies. The air space above Kyiv was still being heavily contested between the defenders and the invaders. Neither side was willing to give the other air superiority.

There was very little time to organize serious defences over this past day, so the soldiers and a few volunteers put up some makeshift defences and barricades, mainly by placing big vehicles on the roads to make it harder for the military vehicles of the invaders to pass through.

Oleksiy and his friend Dmytro were standing on one of the main streets in Kyiv, weapons in hands. Many other men were there too, volunteering to fight and defend their dear city. They knew the Russian soldiers were practically on the doorstep now and would reach Kyiv within hours. It was terrifying. And to make it all worse, it was very cold and windy. Oleksiy could feel his fingers going slightly numb whilst clutching the gun in his hands. He was glad he put on a warm jumper and a fleece on top and wore a beanie hat. This could be a long night and he needed to keep as warm as possible.

"How are you holding up, brother?" Dmytro asked, snapping Oleksiy from his internal contemplation.

"Scared of course," Oleksiy admitted with full honesty.

"Me too," Dmytro nodded. "I'd bet that every one of us here is scared, but we're all united by a common purpose."

"That's true."

"Your family got to the border yet?"

"They're in Lviv right now. There are huge crowds and queues at the train station. They decided to spend the night in the city and attempt to cross the border tomorrow."

"Glad they got far away from here in time. Wish my Liliya was with them."

Oleksiy knew that Dmytro was really worried for his wife and would do anything to protect her. He understood that most men here did not want to fight but had to for the sake of their families and loved ones. Taking up arms and fighting was the lesser evil when the alternative was to see your family get hurt.

"What about you, fella? Do you have a family here?" Dmytro turned to a man who was standing next to him. The man looked about 50 years of age and was of average height. Clearly wasn't a soldier.

"Yeah," the man responded. "Have a wife here and a daughter who lives in Mykolaiv."

"Damn. I heard things are pretty bad in Mykolaiv right now."

"It's true. I worry for my Solomiya greatly, but she's firm in her purpose to save people. She's a nurse and I'm proud of her."

"I hope she stays safe there," Oleksiy spoke with encouragement. "I hope all of us stay protected from the worst."

The man nodded in agreement and Dmytro put his hand on Oleksiy's shoulder reassuringly. They were all in this together, brothers in arms, ready to face the incoming nightmare side by side, shoulder to shoulder.

Minutes and hours went by. Oleksiy spent all that time virtually on the same spot, having nothing more than a couple of protein bars to keep the hunger at bay. He wished that the whole night would go by like this and be uneventful. It was much more preferable for him to worry about cold and boredom than actual fighting. However, soon he could hear more shelling somewhere in the distance, as well as sharp popping noises of gunshots. This meant that the enemies were on the outskirts of the city already and they were coming here. They were getting closer and a big fight was inevitable.

Chapter 2

26th of February
Mykolaiv

Solomiya was helping the soldiers to set up a medical tent during the night. The invaders were approaching Mykolaiv and all the preparations had to be done to ensure the assault would be repelled. Being a nurse, she was usually working at the hospitals. However, now with the war having started, she and many other healthcare workers were expected to work in medical tents closer to the fighting on some occasions. She was mentally prepared for that and she understood perfectly how difficult this would be, because people like her were necessary and had an important job to do – to save lives. Moreover, her beloved Tymur was serving in the army, and being closer to him when he was going fighting was exactly what she wanted.

"I think we've got everything set up," Solomiya sat down next to Tymur.

"You're worrying. I can see it," he replied. "Just take a deep breath, ok?"

"I try, but it will take some time for me to get used to this. My mind is still panicking from the fact that we're being invaded in full."

Tymur gave her a gentle hug and a kiss on the head. Solomiya always felt easier when she was close to him. But now she was worrying not only about the war itself but also for him and his wellbeing. He would be out there fighting and risking his life. She couldn't stand the thought of losing him or even the thought of him being injured or in pain.

"All right, I think it's time that I have to go," Tymur said and got up from his seat.

"Already?"

"Yeah. I have to join with the others. We need to go over our tactics before the enemy gets here."

"Are you anxious?"

"A fair bit, but it's normal to be anxious at a time like this."

"Ok, my dear. Well, I'll be working here for most of today and tomorrow. If you get hurt, you come here so I can take care of you."

Tymur smiled. He always did when Solomiya was being overly caring. To her this was a sign that he heard her clearly and approved. They gave each other a warm kiss and a tight hug; then Tymur picked up his gear and left. Solomiya watched as he continued down the street, glancing back at her every now and again, and once he disappeared around the corner, she went back into the tent.

The tent was spacious and had six beds in it, as well as a lot of medical equipment. There were a couple of other nurses in there too, checking to see if all the medical supplies were sufficient. Solomiya was anticipating the difficulties to come. She knew that within the next day there would be many injured soldiers and possibly civilians too being delivered to her care. Many of them would be hurt quite critically. Some would likely be beyond saving and would pass away on an operating table. And all this would take a huge mental toll on her. But someone had to do this job, someone had to be there to save injured people, and she knew this was her life's purpose, now at a time like this more than ever.

26th of February

Kyiv

Many moving flashes of light appeared in the sky above Kyiv. The barrage of missiles of the invaders was coming down. Oleksiy saw a few buildings in the distance get hit, erupting in huge fires. The chaos of sounds all around was overwhelming, ranging from distant explosions, to gunfire, to people yelling. Oleksiy closed his eyes for a moment, trying to cope with it all, clutching the gun close to his chest.

"You ok there, brother?" Dmytro's voice emerged from this turbulent sea of noises.

"I feel like the whole sky is falling. This is the end for us all, isn't it?" Oleksiy said as he sharply opened his eyes and turned to see his friend standing next to him.

"No, brother. We'll not let it happen. Stay close to me, ok?"

Oleksiy nodded and looked ahead from his cover at the far distance down the street where most of the fighting appeared to be happening, although it was hard to make out exactly what was going on. He hadn't seen any enemy soldiers or machines come through yet, but it was evident that fighting was happening somewhere ahead. There were many checkpoints set up to try and impede the enemy forces, so it was likely that the assailants were being held up at one of those.

Minutes went by and the outbursts of fighting ahead and missiles flying through the night sky continued, but nobody came through yet. A little light of hope sprung up in Oleksiy's mind. Perhaps the invaders wouldn't make it through the defences of the city. Perhaps things weren't so bad. Perhaps the city was stronger and more united than he thought. Afterall, the president chose to stay in Kyiv despite the danger, and this was a huge morale boost for all the citizens, who would be willing to stand together in the face of adversity.

Then he saw a lone vehicle coming along the road from the distance. One of the Russian military vehicles must've broken through the defences ahead and was coming closer. Oleksiy prepared for the confrontation, even though he knew the gun he held in his hands would be no use against an armoured vehicle.

He didn't get a chance to finish that thought when he saw one of the soldiers nearby shoot from one of those Javelin anti-tank weapons that other countries had provided to Ukraine. The Javelin rocket hurtled through the air, leaving behind a trail of smoke, and struck the incoming armoured vehicle with ferocity. A booming noise echoed all over the place as the armoured vehicle burst into dazzling flames and its debris was flung several metres into the air. It was both frightening and magnificent.

"They were barbecued!" Dmytro exclaimed. "Let that be a lesson to any of them for daring to come here!"

Oleksiy felt the same elation Dmytro was feeling. It felt great to see the enemy get destroyed. Even though it was just one vehicle, the spectacular and devastating nature of its destruction was uplifting.

Over the next two hours the noises of fighting ahead diminished and there were fewer missiles coming down from the skies too. By the morning hours there were barely any signs of fighting remaining. It appeared that this particular battle was slowing down and the defences of Kyiv held off the attackers. It felt like a miracle. Oleksiy was expecting a battery of Russian tanks to force its way into Kyiv one way or another during the night, but this did not occur. Perhaps it was too early to celebrate, but this first crucial battle was won and that meant a lot. It meant that the enemy was not as unstoppable as everyone believed. Over the course of just one night, the seemingly inevitable now came under question, and that meant that Ukraine still had a fighting chance.

Oleksiy was really exhausted. Even though he did not engage directly in any of the confrontations, he was waging a battle among his thoughts the entire night and this sapped him off his energy. The rollercoaster of emotions was too much to handle, ranging from utter hopelessness at the start of the night to a thrilling elation after seeing one of Russian armoured vehicles blasted into smithereens.

"Looks like we're dismissed for now," Dmytro returned to Oleksiy after speaking to a few soldiers some distance away. "The orcs are retreating!"

Dmytro and a few other men around seemed to love using the slang term 'orcs' to describe Russian invaders, likely due to the merciless and barbaric nature these invaders showed.

"That's great news!" Oleksiy was glad to hear a confirmation of his observations.

"We gave them hell and we'll do it again!"

"Next time there might be more of them though, so we shouldn't get ahead of ourselves."

"Yes, but next time we'll be even better prepared. How are you feeling anyway?"

"I'm really tired and sleepy," Oleksiy admitted. "I'll probably collapse onto my bed when I return home."

"And you'd be right to do that. You deserved your rest today, brother, as did we all."

The two of them said their goodbyes for now and headed their separate ways back home. The sky was getting brighter now and the morning was here. Oleksiy couldn't help but wonder what most citizens of Kyiv were thinking about as they were waking up. Perhaps they would be in the same state of disbelief as he was, realising that the city still stood and the Russian forces were repelled successfully. Perhaps many were having a sleepless night because of the situation the city was in.

Oleksiy had to take a bus to get him closer to the region where he lived, and after some more walking on foot, he was back home in his apartment. Except now, for the past two days, the apartment was empty. His mum and sister were no longer there. He was all alone. He walked over to one of the cabinets in the living room. A few photos were standing atop it. He picked up the photo that was in the middle and gazed at it. The photo was from many years ago, of him, his sister, his mother and also his father. During all these years the non-stop wars had splintered his family. First his father was taken away from them when Donbas was first attacked, and now he was separated from his mother and sister with no clue of when he'd see them again.

Oleksiy set the photo back down to where it initially was, the thoughts of his family refusing to leave him. He was feeling very low on strength and energy, like a battery that was totally depleted. His feet were moaning and aching from standing all night long, his eyes were heavy, and he was feeling lightheaded. He thought he'd be hungry, but after what he'd just been through, his insides were still tense and in knots and he couldn't intake any food whilst that was the case. He urgently needed a rest, to let go off everything that was happening, at least for just a few hours.

26th of February
Kherson

Taras was sitting in one of the abandoned buildings and aiming down the street through a sniper rifle scope. There had already been a few confrontations on the outskirts of Kherson over the past two days, with the enemy gradually taking more and more territory, so Taras joined in to help the military. During his normal day-to-day life he was a policeman and so he was familiar with using firearms. Physically he was built for fighting too and could face most criminals in a one-on-one fight if the situation called for it. However, normally he handled shoplifters, street brawlers and small-time criminals, and that was significantly less dangerous than what he signed himself up for this time. Despite that, he understood perfectly well that the country needed people like him to act and help the army, because the enemy was much more numerous and better armed.

A couple of enemy soldiers emerged from behind some buildings. Taras spotted them whilst scanning the area with the sniper scope. He signalled for another sniper who was in the same room about the positions of the enemy so that they could coordinate their attack.

After a handful of seconds of carefully aiming and waiting for the right opportunity, Taras shot the enemy soldier down. His ally momentarily shot down the next soldier. Their coordinated attack was a success. However, Taras noticed that the enemy soldiers coming from this direction were in a much smaller number than in the early morning hours. It was starting to look that fewer and fewer enemy soldiers were coming this way. Perhaps they were repelled from this direction or they were preparing a larger assault. Taras and his ally waited for another hour, carefully observing the entire area within their view, and when nobody else was coming through this way, they decided to head downstairs and regroup with the others.

When outside the building, Taras approached the squad commander to get some information on the situation.

"They've pulled back for now, but many more are coming from across the river," the commander told him. "We may have to retreat further into the city."

Taras did not like the sound of those news, but he could perfectly comprehend what they were up against. Defending in smaller settlements was difficult as the cover advantage was minimal. In the city it was easier to set up checkpoints and bottlenecks where the effect of big enemy numbers was diminished. He simply nodded to the commander and then went inside one of the buildings where he could make a call through a secure phoneline. He was checking up on his family every day since the invasion began, even though they were already out of Ukraine and in safety.

"Hello. Taras, is this you?" a woman's voice came through the phone. That was Taras' wife Viktoria.

"Yes. How are you today, Vika? Is everything good?"

"It's all fine over here."

"And the boys? How are they feeling after all this?"

"A little bit sad, but they understand everything. I think they'll get through this with no problems. What about you? I heard there were battles in Kherson already."

"Yes, but so far we can handle it," Taras proclaimed with confidence. He couldn't give any more details of where he was stationed for the sake of national security at a critical time like this, but he wanted to assure his wife that he was fine.

"We are praying for your safety every day, dear Taras. Please look after yourself," Viktoria's voice was very gentle but persuasive.

"I will do my best," he promised.

After he ended the call and felt reassured that his wife and kids were safe and secure, he went back outside. It was likely that there would be no more fighting in this area for the rest of the day, but if what his commander said was true, then the next few days would prove to be very challenging. He wanted to be mentally ready for anything the enemy would throw their way. He knew he needed even to be prepared for defeat.

Danyil and Lera were in a large bomb shelter with many rooms along with several other people. There was a tremendous amount of shelling going on in Mariupol over the past few days, so it was safer to simply stay in the bomb shelter all day and all night for the time being and to bring as many supplies down there as possible. People set up beds, tables and kitchenette areas. The bombing of the city was almost non-stop and was hitting various regions of it, as though someone was choosing a location to bomb completely at random, and therefore most parts of the city were in serious danger. Some of the bombing could be heard and felt in the shelter from time to time, but the people there were trying to occupy themselves and pay less attention to the terrible sounds coming from above.

Because of the constant shelling, there were frequent power cuts and lights would often go off. To cope with that, people in the shelter lit up many candles in each room so that they had plenty of light.

"I'm really worried for mum and dad," Danyil said to Lera whilst they were both sitting on one of the beds in a large room and looking through their phones. "There's been no word from them at all ever since they left."

"Do you think something happened to them?" Lera turned to him straight away. Her facial expression gave away that she was worrying excessively for them.

"I don't know. Maybe it's a signal issue. Phone lines and internet have been cutting out frequently. Maybe they just can't reach us."

Although Danyil said that to calm his sister and he knew this was a reasonable possibility, he still had doubts and was expecting the worst. This was a full-on war and people were going to die in it. His parents were not invincible, and so their lives were at risk.

"Would their superiors tell us if something happened to our parents?" Lera asked after a brief pause.

"I hope they would. The fact they hadn't contacted us is giving me some hope that mum and dad might still be ok."

And again Danyil said that and understood it was a reasonable assumption to make, he still was struggling to believe in those words. The feeling of hope was gradually abandoning him, one little piece at a time.

One of the young women at the other corner of the room began playing a guitar and singing "Oi u luzi chervona kalyna", which was a well-known patriotic Ukrainian song. Two other people in the room joined in on the singing, trying to keep up a more positive and hopeful atmosphere in the shelter and wishing for this nightmare to end as soon as possible.

Danyil listened to the song for a bit, but it was hitting him deeply and making him want to cry. He turned to his sister again.

"Hey, want to get some hot tea or something? It's getting cold again."

"Yeah, I'd love to," Lera agreed.

They got off the bed, walked around the other beds in the room and went into the next room that had a kitchenette area with food and drinks. Danyil picked up one of the kettles that was there and filled it with water. Because there was no electricity at that moment in time, he had to place the kettle over one of the smaller candles so that the fire from the candle would heat up the water. It was going to take a while, so he began gazing around the room. Everyone was trying to quietly get on with something to pass the time. Three kids were playing with toys just a couple of metres away from where Danyil and Lera were standing. Their parents were close by, having a conversation. Another adult, an older man, had his hands together and eyes closed, praying. Two women not far from him were sitting and playing chess with each other.

"Danyil," Lera began after a minute and Danyil turned his gaze towards her, "how are you feeling after having to say goodbye to Dasha?"

"It hurts," he confessed. "Hurts a lot. But what can I do? She made her choice and I made mine."

"Don't you wish we could've gone with her?"

"Maybe. I don't know what would've been best. It's dangerous out there too. Right now, I don't know if she made it to safety or if something happened to her. And if I keep thinking about it, it will keep killing me slowly."

"I understand. Sorry to bring it up."

"It's ok," Danyil sighed. "My emotions are being torn in multiple directions right now with all that's going on. I don't know what's waiting for us in the next few days. All I do know is that you and I must survive and get through this at all costs."

Lera nodded, although the look on her face was that of sadness and worry.

"Is your phone still ok?" Danyil then asked after checking his own. "I think I'll need to charge mine soon. I'll ask the guys who brought the generator if we could charge our phones."

Danyil could remember that someone brought a portable generator down to the shelter, and this was a suitable backup in case electricity went down, which was exactly what happened.

"Mine needs charging soon too," Lera answered his question. "I wouldn't care so much for it if it wasn't our only way to know if mum and dad are ok."

Danyil agreed and then turned towards the kettle to see if the water was hot yet. He could see the bubbles appearing in the water, indicating that it was starting to boil. He took the kettle off the candle fire and poured hot water into two cups. Lera had already placed the tea bags in them.

"You know what? Let's go and play hangman while we're having our tea," Danyil suggested. "It will be like the good old times and will help us to get our minds off everything."

"Great idea!" Lera enjoyed the sound of his suggestion.

Danyil could remember perfectly that his sister always enjoyed this game when she was a kid. They used to play it for hours, and at times they were even getting their parents enticed to play with them. Playing it together now, like they did many years ago, would help them both to relax, which they both badly needed.

27th of February
Kharkiv

"I think we've got everything," Anton said and closed the boot of the car.

"Great, then we're ready to go," Olesya responded. "Ksenia, are you ready too?"

"Yes, I am."

Ksenia was anxious. Only a few days ago she was normally going about her days at the university. She was staying at Olesya's and Anton's apartment as she had no income and couldn't afford to rent a place. Olesya was her close friend since school and the two of them were going to the same university.

It all changed, however, since the war began. The last three days they spent in the basement, taking cover from all the heavy shelling the city was experiencing. And now with the news of the Russian soldiers having entered parts of the city, they decided it was high time to leave Kharkiv before things got a lot worse. Ksenia was reluctant to leave as she knew it was very dangerous to be outdoors in the city streets at this time while the fighting was still quite intense. However, both Olesya and Anton insisted that now was the only chance and that waiting any longer would only make things more dangerous.

Ksenia sat in the backseat of the car, with Olesya in the passenger seat and Anton was going to drive. Everything was ready and it was time to leave. Ksenia said a quiet prayer just as they moved off, desperately hoping for a safe trip out of the city.

The day was cold and grey. After just three days, Ksenia could see numerous heaps of debris and broken glass on the roads next to damaged buildings. The signs of destruction on the buildings looked like hideous wounds, as though the buildings were alive and screaming from pain, crippled and suffering from sadistic attacks of the invaders. Seeing what was happening to her beloved country, Ksenia's heart was fracturing more and more and she wanted to break down into tears.

Many of the roads were busy and filled with cars and buses. It appeared that many civilians were trying to flee the city. With the considerable amount of bombing happening and the enemy forces now entering the city itself, it was clear that many civilians were scared and wanted to escape. After just a few minutes of driving, they got stuck in a long queue on one of the roads.

"Seems we'll be here a while," Anton declared out loud.

"Just be patient," Olesya tried her best to be optimistic. "Slowly but surely we'll make our way forward."

"Yeah, slowly is indeed the right word."

Anton and Olesya were twins and always lived together, at first with parents, and later just with each other. They often agreed on many things, and when they didn't, they were usually calm about it and always respected each other's opinions.

"Perhaps we should've waited a few more days," Ksenia decided to bring up her suggestion again, hoping that she could still convince them to return and wait it out.

"I dread to think what will be happening here in a few days," came Olesya's reply. "If anything, we should've left before the invasion happened. We should've taken this threat more seriously. But it's fine. It's not too late yet."

"You really think Kharkiv is going to fall to the occupiers?"

"I don't know what to think, but it's possible. We need to prepare for the worst case scenario."

"Right, I think I'm going to turn into a side road," Anton interrupted them. "We might have to go around the queue."

The girls didn't argue and decided to agree with his judgement. Their car along with a few other cars on the road turned to the side road that was just ahead. It seemed to Ksenia that Anton knew the way around these streets, so the chances of them getting lost were slim.

They made a few turns and headed along a narrower road, following a handful of other cars in front. They could make some progress by going down this way, but it was a longer way around. Over time these smaller roads led them to a larger one.

"Looks like we've found a good diversion," Anton felt pleased.

All of a sudden a loud gunfire sound came from somewhere to their left. The car in front of them got hit by what looked like a barrage of machine gun fire, and within moments it swerved aside sharply and toppled over. Before they could react to what they saw, Ksenia heard dozens of ear-piercing impact sounds of bullets striking their car and Anton's car window loudly smashing into pieces. She only caught a quick glimpse of a lone military vehicle at the end of a side road before ducking for cover and holding her hands over her head.

"Oh shit!" Anton exclaimed and slammed hard on the gas pedal to make the car accelerate.

Their car veered sharply around the car at the front, which was now toppled over, and sped through the road to get away from danger.

"I'm hit!" Olesya screamed and clutched her right shoulder, which was now starting to bleed, with blood trickling from between her fingers despite her trying to keep the wound closed. "Anton, you are also hit! Anton!"

"I know!" Anton yelled and continued speeding through the road to make sure the attackers were nowhere near.

"Anton, you have to stop now!"

It seemed that Anton listened to his sister this time round and began slowing the car until it came to an abrupt stop. Anton loudly groaned from pain and opened his car door. Once the door was open, he collapsed onto the ground next to the car as though all strength was gone from him.

"Anton!" his sister cried his name out again.

Ksenia wasted no time and got out of the car as swiftly as she could. She gave a quick look in all directions to make sure no invaders were nearby and then rushed to Anton's side. Olesya was trying to climb towards the driver's seat and to see her brother, but she was struggling and unable to move herself. Ksenia turned Anton onto his back and saw a couple of bullet holes in his chest which were profusely bleeding. Blood was coming from Anton's mouth too and he was choking on it.

"Ksenia, stop..." he spoke barely. "Save my sis..."

"Anton, don't leave us!" Olesya continued screaming from inside of the car, trying to get closer to see him, but her own wound was severely weakening her.

Ksenia felt her heartbeat stop for a moment and a paralyzing shock took over her. Her hands began trembling uncontrollably and she could say nothing at all despite trying hard.

"Anton!" came Olesya's cries as tears flooded down her face. "Ksenia, save him!"

"I… I can't. He's gone, Olesya," Ksenia said so quietly that it sounded almost like a hoarse whisper.

"No! He's not gone!"

Ksenia rushed into the car to check on her best friend. Olesya was trying to unsuccessfully fight her way through the car, but Ksenia stopped her and embraced her tightly to try and soothe her. At that moment there was nothing else they could do but be there for each other. On top of that, time was short and Olesya continued bleeding from her shoulder. They needed to get to a hospital as soon as possible.

28th of February
Mykolaiv

Solomiya was busy working in the medical tent for the third day in a row. The last two days had been extremely tiring for her as she worked for 14 hours straight on the first one and just as many hours on the second, only coming back home to sleep in between. The injured soldiers and civilians kept coming throughout those two days. With what she was witnessing so far, she expected that the present day's shift would also last 14 hours, if not more.

The fighting on the outskirts of Mykolaiv was fierce over the past two days from what she heard. However, the enemy forces failed to hold their ground in the city for long and were pushed out within a day and were now retreating. It was a small bit of relief to know that the city repelled the attack relatively quickly. She didn't know the details of where Tymur was stationed, but he was likely involved in defending the city during that fight. Solomiya hoped that with the enemy retreating, perhaps she'd see Tymur for some time before he would be sent to fight again. She felt that she really needed to see him. These days were like a nightmare for her, with each day being seemingly worse than the one before. Seeing him even for a few minutes would help her to calm down.

Once she finished dressing the wound of the most recently delivered patient, she walked over to check on two others who were in a critical condition. At that moment in time only one other nurse was in the tent to oversee the patients. There were a few medical tents set up within the area and at times nurses in one tent had to go and help those in another tent. There was barely any down time for them to catch their breath.

Moments later she heard a vehicle pull up nearby. This usually meant one thing – more injured patients were being delivered. She braced herself for what was to come. She began to wonder what kind of injuries she would see this time. In just the last two days she already managed to see a person with third-degree burns on his face, as well as a soldier who lost both of his legs.

The doors of the vehicle that had just arrived slammed and Solomiya could hear footsteps and something being dragged out. A tall, middle-aged soldier entered the tent and swiftly scanned around it. His eyes stopped on Solomiya.

"Are you Solomiya Kovalchuk?" he asked

"Yes, that's me," Solomiya responded, feeling puzzled and curious to know what he wanted.

"We have some news."

Oh no. That's never a good phrase to hear during a war. Something must've happened to Tymur. Those thoughts were racing through her head. Fear wrapped its long, spindly arms around her in a tight embrace. She slowly walked closer to the soldier. He motioned with his head and stepped out of the tent. Solomiya followed him out.

"You were listed as his next of kin," the soldier said and pointed at the body bag that was taken out of the ambulance. "Condolences for your loss."

Solomiya's eyes widened and her face lost all the colour. She felt as though a literal bullet struck her in the chest. Her stomach began twisting into a knot and she could not take a breath in. A sharp sense of vertigo hit her hard and everything around her began to blur together.

With each step that was shaking beyond her control she approached the body bag and knelt down beside it. Her trembling hands stretched out so that she could unzip it. And just as she feared most, she saw the face of her beloved. There was no life in him anymore. Stains of blood and dried up dirt were all over his face. She couldn't look further down to see the condition of the rest of his body, except that there was a lot of blood and dirt covering his ragged clothes.

"A tank shell landed right by his feet," the soldier reported in a bleak tone of voice. "He died instantly."

Solomiya felt her insides being torn to pieces. Her heart was being ripped right out of her chest and tossed into a scorching fire. Her hands were turning ice-cold and her eyes could not see much anymore because they were being drowned by her tears.

She began crying uncontrollably and felt no strength to resist at all. Whilst crying, she lowered herself down to where her beloved lay and pressed her face against his, clutching onto him with both hands, refusing to let him go, even though she knew that this would not bring him back. The tears would not stop streaming down her face. The throbbing pain in her chest only continued getting heavier, pounding her akin to heavy punches. She wished she was there with him in his final moments. She wished that she would've died together with him. And now he was gone and she was left behind all by herself. One question kept repeating itself in her head non-stop. *What am I supposed to do now without you?*

Chapter 3

1ˢᵗ of March
Kharkiv

Ksenia finished talking to her mother on the phone, who had been checking up on her every day since the invasion began. The past two days she spent at a hospital, although she miraculously was unscathed after one of the invader vehicles opened fire on her and her friends. Her friend Olesya on the other hand was being treated and had to get plenty of rest. Ksenia was staying by her friend's side during these two days. She couldn't leave Olesya by herself without a friendly face close by, and she was also increasingly scared to go back to the apartment to be on her own. It was best to stay together with her friend.

Sleeping wasn't easy in the hospital, with the lack of space and constant noise, but these were the least of her concerns. Mentally she was still shaken after what happened, especially witnessing the sight of Anton getting killed in such violent way. She kept having nightmares for the past two nights. In the nightmare she was seeing herself and Olesya driving in a car, only for a spray of bullets to come out of nowhere and hit them both. Each time she found herself waking up in cold sweat and a racing heartbeat.

After putting her phone in one of her jacket pockets and taking a deep breath in, she headed back to the ward where Olesya was. She usually stayed close to it and hadn't even left the same floor for the past two days. Olesya was peacefully sleeping when Ksenia entered the room, so she decided not to disturb her friend and simply sat down on a chair nearest the bed where her friend lay.

Her gaze diverted to the screen of a TV in the room. News were showing the most recent Russian attack on their country – a missile hitting the Freedom Square in Kharkiv city centre. Seeing the clips of destruction from that missile were making Ksenia really sorrowful and wanting to cry. *Why are they trying to wipe us out? Why did we deserve this?* These were some of the questions she kept asking herself. Thankfully the invaders were quickly pushed out of the city over the past day, but they were still attempting to surround it and kept continuously shelling it, and this made life in Kharkiv exceedingly dangerous.

"Hey, how are you, Ksenia?" Olesya's voice came.

Ksenia turned over her shoulder and saw that Olesya was already awake.

"I'm ok, dear. How are you feeling?" Ksenia diverted the question back as she felt Olesya's condition was much more important to discuss.

"I'm recovering. Just the shoulder feels a bit... I don't know, hard to move."

"Just give it time and don't strain it. I'm sure once it's fully healed, you'll be able to move with it freely again."

"Yeah," Olesya agreed and went silent.

"Have you also been having nightmares these past two nights?" Ksenia changed the topic.

"Last night I did, yeah. Saw us three trying to run down a road whilst the invaders shot at us."

"A bit similar to what I've been seeing too."

"I miss Anton. I can't believe he's gone," Olesya began crying. "It was all my fault. I should've listened to you that it was too dangerous to try and leave the city."

"No, don't say that. None of us could've known what could happen in the city. We were all trying to do what was best – we were all trying to stay alive."

"You're right. It's those barbaric occupiers that we need to blame. The damned orcs they are! The fascists took my brother from me and brought so much violence and despair to our peaceful country. They all deserve to be in hell!"

Ksenia could feel her friend's anger and despair. She felt the same emotions and wished she could do something to change the situation. But she could also understand that she alone could not do much and this was making her feel hopeless and defenceless. She realised that within just a few days, her life was no longer in her control and was fully dependent on the larger circumstances in the entire country.

"By the way," she suddenly remembered, "the hospital mentioned that they got in contact with your dad and that he will be coming here."

Olesya nodded to show that she understood and then gazed at the TV screen to see the devastation that was being shown on the news.

"Want me to get you something to eat?" Ksenia said as she got off the chair.

"I don't have much hunger, but I won't object. Need to make myself eat if I want to recover soon."

"All right, I'll be right back then."

"Thanks, Ksenia. I appreciate you being here for me."

Ksenia smiled feebly and then walked over to the door and left the room to try and get them both something to eat.

1st of March

Kyiv

Oleksiy was at Dmytro's house. Dmytro's wife Liliya cooked some traditional Ukrainian meals with the ingredients they had at home. Food choices were limited in Kyiv these days, but Liliya did her best with what was at home. Liliya was always very homely and enjoyed the simple things that created a cosy atmosphere for those around her. The last few days had been hard and depressing in Kyiv, and air raid alarms kept coming on and off throughout the entire time, even during the nights, so a little bit of positive time with dear people was essential for staying strong and motivated.

"Is Vadym coming as well?" Oleksiy asked his friend.

"Yes, he said he would. Although he sounded off," Dmytro answered. "I could hear sadness in his voice, but he didn't tell me anything."

"This war has affected all of us, so he must be going through a very hard time too."

Liliya brought some more food at this point, set it on the table and then sat down.

"Eat as much as you like, Oleksiy. Don't be shy," she said.

"Thank you."

"Hope you're feeling better after the fighting on our city's doorstep. Dmytro told me it was pretty fierce."

"Yeah. It was a huge relief that the city held on. I can't really say that I contributed much though. I've not fired a single shot," Oleksiy explained modestly.

"Neither have I," Dmytro admitted, "but we've all stood together and beaten the enemy back, and that's what counts, brother."

"I agree with you 100 percent," Oleksiy said as he put a few vareniki on his plate. "I am sure all of us will be ready to spend the whole night defending the city again should the need arise."

All three of them got lost in thoughts here, reflecting on the events of the last few days and still trying to accept it as their new reality. A part of Oleksiy still felt as though it was all just a bad dream, a dream he couldn't wake up from. He was still trying to cope with the fact that the horrors of war had come back to haunt him after 8 years and that this time it was a lot worse and a lot more was at stake.

"I'm going to be helping to set up the defences in the city," Oleksiy stated after the silence. "Every single one of us counts. I think only through mutual effort we'll be able to beat back the occupiers."

"I'm going to be right there with you," Dmytro acknowledged. "No orc will dare set foot in Kyiv. Not on my watch."

A second later there was a knock on their apartment door.

"This must be Vadym," Liliya said and got up to open the door.

Their apartment was rather modest in size and the front door was just within a few steps from the dining room. Liliya opened the door, and as they expected, it was Vadym – Oleksiy's and Dmytro's boss at the car garage shop. Vadym was in his late 40s, but at this moment he looked like he was a good ten years older. Grief and anxiety were all over his face.

"Vadym, what happened?" Liliya asked before he even stepped in.

He went inside, took his hat off and briefly closed his eyes so he could muster up the strength to speak.

"My children in Kharkiv came under fire from a Russian military vehicle. My son Anton died and my daughter Olesya is now in a hospital."

Tears rolled down his face after saying that. It looked like the news hit him really hard, as they would hit any person who loses a child. He sat down by the table next to Dmytro, looking downwards the entire time and struggling to stay strong. Oleksiy and Dmytro saw Vadym more as a good friend than a boss and it was normal for them to share personal problems with each other.

"I'm sorry. I didn't want to bring in more problems. We were supposed to be having an enjoyable evening together," he apologised.

"Hey, we understand that. It is best that you're here with us at this horrendous time," Oleksiy responded.

"Yeah, horrendous indeed. I should've been there with them."

"It's not your fault," Liliya tried to console him.

Oleksiy couldn't imagine in how much mental pain Vadym was at this moment. He remembered the time when he lost his father and how hard it hit him and his whole family, how much they cried and how empty their lives felt. But to lose children must've been even harder and much more difficult to bear.

"Listen, Dmytro, Oleksiy, I'll be leaving to Kharkiv from tomorrow morning to be with my daughter," Vadym declared. "I'd like to leave you two in charge of our car garage in my absence. Once it gets safe enough to re-open it, feel free to do so. And if the army requires any tools or spare parts to help in the city's defences, you give them anything they need. Do anything that will help to kill as many of those bastards that have attacked us and came to kill our children."

Oleksiy and Dmytro both agreed and showed their understanding. Keeping the city safe was the priority at that moment, because their business wouldn't be able to function properly until the safety of the citizens was re-established and some form of peace was back in the country.

"Will you be ok driving on your own?" Dmytro asked after a few moments, "Your blood pressure must be in the danger zone after today's news."

"I have no choice but to be ok," Vadym replied. "For my daughter's sake, I have to get there by any means and to support her."

Oleksiy admired Vadym's persistence in the face of so many problems and danger. He reminded him of his own father, who also never gave up, no matter how hard something was. Oleksiy intended to be the same way. He had good role models in his life and he wanted to follow their example, to prove to himself that he was strong and could endure no matter what the world threw at him.

2nd of March
Kherson

Over the last few days, the fighting in Kherson moved further inward into the city. Taras continued to help the military in an attempt to impede enemy progress. He did not know how much longer they would be able to hold the invaders off, but he intended to take out as many of them as possible, even if they took the city eventually. He wished for some backup to come and help, but he realised that other cities were also struggling and there simply were not enough soldiers to stop this gargantuan enemy force.

He and several other soldiers were taking cover behind buildings and barricades along one of the city streets on the outskirts of the city. Russian forces were at the other end of the street. Taras could see several tanks approaching and braced himself for another fierce confrontation with the attackers.

"Get those NLAWs and Javelins here!" one of the soldiers shouted, trying to get someone to bring the anti-tank weapons forward.

A few soldiers ran in, carrying what was requested. There weren't enough anti-tank weapons for all the tanks that were getting nearer. It looked to Taras that they might be needing to retreat again. Their forces were spread out too thinly and the enemy appeared to be having an infinite number of troops to throw at them.

The enemy tanks were even closer now. A couple of them fired at the barricades, causing massive and deafening explosions at the places where their shells landed. The soldiers that had anti-tank weapons now stepped forward and were preparing to fire them at the tanks when the unit commander came and yelled to stop. *What? Why should we stop?* Taras was confused for a moment when he heard the command.

"Orders from the top," the commander spoke once everyone ceased shooting and things got quieter. "The city has been surrounded by the enemy and we are to lay down our arms and surrender."

"No way!" Taras yelled out loud, unable to stop himself.

"We have no choice. These are our orders and we will obey them," the commander responded to Taras' outburst.

Taras turned back to face the enemy forces. Some of the infantry now appeared in sight too, emerging from behind the tanks. The enemy really was too numerous. The choice became quite clear – either they surrendered or they got slaughtered by the enemy forces.

A few of the Ukrainian defenders began to lay down their arms. Taras was reluctant to do the same as he really wanted to kill as many of the invaders as possible, but now was not the best time and it was better to surrender, so he did.

The next few minutes were tense and full of despondency as the Russian soldiers surrounded them from all sides and had them discard all weapons, ammo and grenades they had with them. The enemy had them and the whole city captive, and Taras knew that there was nothing more he could do about it other than simply accept the outcome. Kherson was lost.

Solomiya was back to working in a hospital. She was given the last two days off to mourn the death of her beloved and today she was expected to come back to work. To her two days were nowhere near enough to pick herself up after losing Tymur. Her mental suffering only got worse because she was all alone these days and for the first time felt the lack of her beloved nearby, with the dreadful reality setting in that he was gone forever.

Now that she was at work, she tried to put on a brave face. She tied her long dark hair in a ponytail, made sure her uniform was clean and tidy, and reached the ward where she was told to work today. Some of the hospital corridors were full with people, waiting to be treated for their injuries or their pre-existing conditions. With the sharp influx of patients, the doctors and nurses were too overworked and couldn't manage to see everyone on time.

Solomiya stopped briefly in one of the empty corridors, closing her eyes and trying to stay strong. She felt that her whole mental state was being held together just with toothpicks and rubber bands and would fall apart at any moment. During some moments the intensity of feelings would increase, and then after some time they would subside. During moments of heightened emotions, Solomiya felt crippled and unable to do anything. She simply had to stop doing everything, close her eyes and fight with her inner self.

"Solomiya, how are you feeling, dear? I've heard what happened to Tymur. I am so sorry," a familiar voice came from behind her.

Solomiya turned around and saw her friend Nadiya who was also working at this hospital as a nurse. Nadiya was only slightly older, and the two of them had many common interests and often talked to each other whenever they had breaks from work. Upon seeing Nadiya, Solomiya felt a little easier. It was pleasant to see a friendly face.

"I'm managing," Solomiya gave a brief response whilst wiping away a tear that was rolling down her cheek.

"If you ever need to get anything off your mind, I am always here to listen," Nadiya tried to comfort her.

"Thank you, Nadiya. You're a wonderful friend. I hope everything is fine with your family."

"More or less, yes. Although I'll likely be going to Kropyvnytskyi in a few days where they live. They need help and support."

Kropyvnytskyi was a city a few hours north of Mykolaiv, closer to the central parts of Ukraine. Solomiya realised her friend would be somewhat far away and they probably wouldn't see each other for a while.

"Are you going to stay there long?" Solomiya was curious as she hoped for her friend to not be gone for a long time.

"Honestly don't know. It depends on how much help my parents need. I'll likely be working there for the time being. But I hope to come back here soon. All of my friends are here."

"I'll miss you greatly, but I understand. Your family really needs you and you should be with them at a difficult time like this."

"Thanks, Solomiya. Let's stay in contact whilst I'm away. At a time like this, we all need to stick together."

"I'd like that very much. You know, I've been in my thoughts a lot these days and I realised something very important," Solomiya stated with a hint of a contemplative expression on her face. "There is a separate battle within each of us. For some of us, who lost their loved ones in this war, this battle is harder, but the outcome is all the same. We can only achieve victory if we manage to rise over the darkness in us. And to do that alone without support of loved ones is just incredibly hard."

"I agree with you completely. We'll pull through this together. Ukraine will pull through this."

On that note Nadiya continued with her work duties and Solomiya began hers. Solomiya knew it was going to be a very tough shift to get through on an emotional level and that there would be many moments of weakness. Her mind would not be fully focused on her work most of the time, but she was prepared to fight through all the pain and do whatever she could to move forward one day at a time.

Today will be very hard, but tomorrow will be a little bit better, and day after even better than that. She knew she merely needed to stay strong until time healed the gaping wound in her heart. She didn't know how long it would take. Perhaps it wouldn't fully heal at all. But it had to get better than now. It had to.

3rd of March
Mariupol

The last 24 hours were some of the worst. Danyil and Lera could hear a lot of shelling going on above. It seemed like the shelling was unending for many hours straight. The thoughts of seeing the city after all of that were frightening Danyil, so he kept trying to push them away.

Now that the shelling had stopped and it had been quiet for a couple of hours, several people in the same shelter decided to go up above and to restock on supplies, as the food and water were running low inside the shelter.

"We should go as well. We've been boxed in here all week," Danyil suggested to his sister.

"Just give me a moment. I need to clear my thoughts. I'm really worried about mum and dad," Lera said whilst looking down at the floor.

The last message Danyil received on his phone was over a day ago and it was an update that their parents had gone missing. After that the batteries in both of their phones had died and they were unable to recharge them. There was no electricity in the shelter all these days, and the portable generator to provide electricity during the blackouts was depleted by now with everyone needing to use it.

"I know, sis. I worry for them too. I just hope and pray to God that they're still alive."

"And now we'll never know, because we'll not be able to charge our phones."

"They will probably inform us some other way," Danyil tried to be a little hopeful and to encourage his sister. He had to try to keep her motivated and not give up as he hated seeing her depressed.

"All right. Let's just go outside and get some more food. The enemies will likely continue shelling us again soon and I'd rather be back here when that happens," Lera got up from the chair and joined her brother.

They gently walked up the stairs and past a couple of doors till they were outside. It was late morning time by the looks of it. The residential buildings in front of them that stood opposite to the shelter entrance were in a terrible shape. There were enormous pitch black char marks all over them, holes and chunks missing in some of the walls, and huge heaps of rocky debris laying at their feet. And there was smoke and soot in every inch of the air. It all looked as though a tsunami of fire had passed through the area and left its hideous scorch marks on the buildings.

They briskly walked past the first few buildings on the way to their own apartment block. It too was in a similar shape as the buildings they had just seen. Some of the walls that they passed were full of small holes, indicating that they were peppered with shrapnel when the bombing was happening. A shudder overtook Danyil when seeing shrapnel marks in the buildings as he immediately imagined the sensation of getting hit by shrapnel flying at deadly speeds and wedging in flesh and bone.

"Danyil, look," Lera pointed a few floors up.

She was pointing at where their apartment was. Danyil's eyes widened as he now saw a horrendously big hole in the building instead of the familiar balcony that used to be there.

"Our apartment," Danyil barely spoke out, feeling like he was about to throw up.

Lera began crying her eyes out after seeing the state of the building, realising that their apartment was no more. Danyil put both of his arms around her to try and console her, even though he was feeling just as weak and wished someone would console him instead. *What sort of monsters would do this?* It was so hard to accept that just a few days ago this whole neighbourhood was whole and intact and peaceful, and now it was charred and in ruins. Now it became unliveable, in a matter of just a few days.

"We need to go up there and see what survived," he then suggested. "Maybe we can grab a few more of our belongings."

Lera agreed without saying anything and the two of them went into the building and headed up the stairs. There were numerous stones and pieces of broken walls scattered all over the stairs, so they had to be careful as they were ascending. The dust that filled the air inside the building was irritating to the eyes and throat. Danyil found himself needing to cough a few times in order to clear his throat.

Once they reached their front door, Danyil unlocked it and pushed it open. He could see that Lera was turning away and was apprehensive to be greeted with a sight of destruction. As the door swung open, Danyil peered inside. He could barely recognize their apartment. It looked completely different to what it was like just a few days ago.

Lera followed him inside and mustered up the courage to see what happened. Her eyes were wide open in shock and tears were coming down from them. Half of the kitchen was gone, as was half of the living room. One of the bedrooms was gone completely. It was the bedroom where their parents had slept. Danyil couldn't help but notice the parallel between their parents being missing and the bedroom where their parents had slept also being gone. It felt like the universe was trying to tell him something, to send him the news that their parents would never return. He refused to believe it, but seeing his parents' belongings swept away into oblivion was not making it any easier to deny a bitter possibility.

Both of them walked a bit further along their destroyed apartment, being careful with each step in case the floor was unstable. To their surprise, their bedroom was still fully intact, likely because it was further inside the building. However, standing in the centre of the living room, Danyil could see the remains of the apartment above them through a massive hole in the ceiling, as well as the remains of the apartment below as half of the floor was missing.

And in front, when looking outside through the empty space where walls used to be and seeing more neighbourhoods, all that Danyil and Lera could see were signs of relentless aggression and destruction. Entire neighbourhoods were in ruins, each building more charred than the one before it, and patches of unsightly smoke everywhere. Next to the buildings were broken cars that now were nothing more than scrap metal, as well as toppled lampposts and trees, scattered all over the roads and sidewalks. It looked like a scene from a post-apocalyptic movie, and yet it was reality, a reality which Danyil and Lera were now living.

"Danyil, they've destroyed our city and our lives. They've destroyed everything!" Lera cried with trembling words.

Danyil gave his sister a hug to try and calm her. He knew that nothing he'd do would change what their city turned into, but he wanted to give some sense of comfort to his sister and make her feel a little safer. After a few moments of crying, Lera continued:

"They are not our brothers. They are monsters! Brotherly nations do not do this to each other. Only savages do. I hope they all die! I hope they all burn in hell for eternity!"

Danyil didn't know what to think of all this, but Lera's words rang true. He couldn't imagine that reasonable and compassionate human beings would rain so much destruction on innocent civilians who posed no threat to anyone.

"Let's take as much as we can," he suggested after a couple of more minutes of contemplation. "We may not return here again, so best to take anything that's useful."

"Ok, and then what?"

"Then we'll go and get some food and return to the shelter. There have been talks that civilian evacuations may happen soon in the days to come. I think it will be best for us to escape the city when the opportunity comes. It's not safe here at all."

Lera didn't say anything and instead just went into their bedroom to look for anything useful such as clothes, shoes, blankets, and so on. Danyil took one more glimpse at the sight in front of him, of the devastated neighbourhood outside, then sighed and went to help his sister.

Chapter 4

4th of March
Somewhere near Kherson

Taras could feel the truck finally coming to a stop. He along with many of the soldiers and volunteers who were defending Kherson were taken as prisoners. He remembered several trucks worth of prisoners, although they were all taken to different places. He couldn't tell where he was taken along with those in the same truck as him. They all were kept in the back of the vehicle with hands tied and bags over their heads.

"Out!" came a stern voice once the back of the truck was opened.

Taras felt someone pick him up with force and drag him out of the truck. Then suddenly the bag over his head was abruptly taken off and he was blinded by the bright light. It took a few seconds for his eyes to adjust to it, and once they did, he saw an old building in front, some sort of abandoned military barracks. He turned in the direction of the truck and saw Russian soldiers taking other prisoners out of the truck too.

When every prisoner was out of the truck, all of the enemy soldiers came together into a small group and faced them.

"Listen up, khokhli!" one of the Russian soldiers began. "This is where you'll spend the next few weeks and possibly the remainder of your miserable lives. Now follow us single file."

The word 'khokhli' that he used was a well-known derogatory term used on Ukrainians. From the moment Taras heard that word, he understood their captors would be treating them with excessive humiliation to try and break their morale. He expected no decency or mercy from them and he knew they would do undignified things to him and the other prisoners.

A handful of the Russian soldiers led the way and the prisoners followed them. The other soldiers kept observing and following behind, making sure no prisoner tried escaping. Every captive person had a beaten expression on the face and many of them were continually looking at the ground.

Once inside the building, there was hardly any natural light. Mostly there were dark corridors and dimly lit rooms. Only the main hallway was well-illuminated as it had windows and a reasonable number of lights. The building as a whole was in a poor state and clearly was not used by anyone for a while. The paint was peeling off of the walls in many places, thick layers of dust were covering the tables and chairs, and there were old cobwebs hanging off parts of a ceiling. It was surprising that there were still a few lights there that even worked.

The prisoners were all gathered in the centre of the main hallway, which was spacious enough for everyone. The Russian soldiers began forcefully shoving a few of the prisoners at the back of the line forwards.

"You're all here, good," one of the Russian soldiers announced. "I hate the fact that we have to look after scum like you, but these are our orders. None of us here is in the mood, so it's in your best interest to behave yourselves and do as you're told. Is that clear?"

There was no response from prisoners. Many were still confused and emotionally down.

"He's talking to you, you piece of shit!" another Russian soldier came from behind the prisoners and slapped one of them in the back of the head.

"Is that clear!?" the first Russian soldier asked in a louder voice.

The prisoners all acknowledged with a simple 'yes' that they understood the rules. The Russian soldier who was giving instructions then carefully looked through all the prisoners and his eyes eventually stopped.

"You two, over here. Your heads need to be shaved."

Two of the female prisoners stepped out of the group. They seemed to be the only women among prisoners. The Russian soldier motioned for them to stand separately and to be taken to another room. Taras was hoping these women would be treated with some sort of decency, but he knew that his hopes were unrealistic and the Russian soldiers would probably hurt and humiliate these women. What was to come in the next few days was anyone's guess. Taras surrendered himself to fate. He had no idea if he'd still be alive, so he chose to think of his family – his wife Vika and their two small boys. He desperately desired to see them again at this difficult moment, wondering if this would ever happen or if he'd never set his eyes upon them again.

Ksenia was sitting by her friend's side. Olesya was laying in the hospital bed and had been making a great recovery over the last few days. She was meant to be discharged from the hospital on this day and was now waiting for her dad Vadym to arrive from Kyiv. Ksenia was supporting Olesya all these days, not leaving the hospital at all and making sure Olesya had everything that she needed. The nightmares continued to torment them both, ruining their sleep and kicking their mental state to the ground each time.

Suddenly a knock on the room's door. Both Ksenia and Olesya turned towards it as it opened. Vadym was here already. As he came in, Ksenia saw Olesya's face light up with a smile - the first time it lit up this whole week. Vadym also looked incredibly elated and relieved to finally see his daughter. As he entered, he walked straight to Olesya's bed. Olesya sat up as much as she could and gave her father a very tight hug, which he returned with the same amount of love. For a moment Ksenia could see tears running down Olesya's face.

"Dad, I missed you so much," said Olesya after wiping the tears off her face.

"I missed you too, darling," Vadym said; tears were running down his face too. "I am so sorry I was not there for you and for Anton."

"It's not your fault, dad. It really isn't. Please don't blame yourself. I'm just relieved you're here now."

Vadym turned to Ksenia at this moment and nodded gently.

"Ksenia, thank you for looking after Olesya all these days. I am sure she couldn't have asked for a better friend."

Ksenia just smiled and felt shy to receive a compliment. She was always ready to help her friends, especially Olesya, who was her closest friend for many years.

"Did you speak to your mum already?" Vadym turned back to Olesya.

"No. I don't even know how to begin. TV in Moscow is likely telling her entirely different things to what is really going on here. I expected for her to phone me first, but she hasn't yet."

"We still should tell her everything. She deserves to know."

"All right. But let's get home first. I'm tired of this hospital room."

Ksenia and Vadym helped Olesya off the hospital bed. Her injured shoulder and arm were still really sore and her range of motion on it was limited, but she could walk fine. Ksenia got hers and her friend's personal belongings and they all left the ward.

Once in the car, Olesya chose to sit in the backseat. She was terrified to be anywhere near the front. Her anxiety was so strong that she was keeping herself low down in her seat, in an almost laying down position. Ksenia could imagine how terrified her friend was. She also felt anxious being in the car again and being driven through the streets of Kharkiv, but she could hold her worries under control. Vadym was driving the car and Ksenia noticed that he was very tired.

"Are you ok?" she asked him. "Maybe it would be better for me to drive?"

"I've not slept much these past two nights," he answered, "but it's fine. I should have no trouble getting us home."

They were driving back to the apartment where Ksenia lived together with Olesya and Anton until recently. Ksenia felt her mind and body being on high alert, carefully observing every street to make sure someone wasn't about to shoot in their direction. She also kept regularly turning towards the backseat and checking on Olesya too. She was greatly worried for her best friend.

The roads they took were mostly clear and they got to their destination a few minutes later. Ksenia breathed a sigh of relief and got out of the car. She looked around again, noticing that it was quiet. A few buildings in the distance were damaged and were likely hit by enemy missiles in the last few days. The neighbourhood around their apartment building, however, was still unharmed.

Vadym helped Olesya out of the car and took her things. Ksenia waited for them and then led the way to the apartment building. The inside of the apartment was just as they left it. Once there, Ksenia felt a little safer and she could see that Olesya was feeling the same way. Although catching glimpse of Anton's belongings was reminding them of that horrible day when he died. Olesya gave Ksenia a hug from the side, holding onto her and burrowing her own head in Ksenia's arm.

"Hey, it will be ok, Olesya," Ksenia said as soon as Olesya hugged her. Olesya was silent. She was obviously missing her brother a great deal.

Vadym brought the rest of the things from the car and closed the front door of the apartment.

A few minutes later, once they managed to make themselves comfortable, Olesya began trying to phone her mother who lived in Moscow. Ksenia could see her friend looking worried and contemplating something, likely wondering how she would start the conversation. Olesya took a couple of deep breaths and then began dialling the number. It took a few attempts for the call to go through, but eventually it succeeded. Olesya put the call on speaker so everyone in the room could hear it.

"Hello?" Olesya's mother Ulyana answered the call.

"Mum, it's me, Olesya."

"Olesya, dear, how are you? I heard something is happening in Ukraine. Are you ok?"

"Not really. There is a war here, mum. The Russian forces are destroying our cities and killing our people."

"That can't be true. It's only a small military operation to get rid of extremists," Ulyana was refusing to believe the news from her daughter.

"I take it Anton was an extremist then? Because you know what? They killed him, mum! He's no more!" Olesya began weeping when she said that.

"Anton was killed? How did it happen?" a tone of fear and sadness was heard in Ulyana's voice.

"We were trying to flee the city and they opened fire on our car."

"I... I don't know what to think, dear. I just wish you two were safe here with me."

"Maybe it would've been better if you were here with us instead."

"Are you sure our people did this? Maybe those Nazis did it. Our people would never attack peaceful civilians. It's not why they went on this operation."

"Think what you want, mum! If you want to believe the propaganda they feed you on TV, then so be it! I only phoned you because you deserve to know about Anton. I won't be calling you again!"

Before her mother could reply to that, Olesya hung up the phone and firmly placed it on the table in front. Tears were still coming down her face. Ksenia put her hand on Olesya's shoulder to show support. Olesya just continued staring at the floor in sadness. Vadym was also speechless and couldn't find the words to say anything. Ksenia thought it was insane that a mother would not believe her child or kept finding excuses for what was happening. *How many lies were they fed over there that they refuse even to believe their children?*

5th of March
Mykolaiv

Solomiya came for her shift at the hospital as normal. The days had started to blur together. The emptiness inside of her after losing Tymur continued to persist. *"What was the point in living?"* she thought. Her country was falling apart, her beloved was gone, and she was on her last threads, fighting on, trying to move forward. But forward to where? To what kind of future?

She needed to focus and push those existential thoughts away. Her superiors mentioned a few minutes earlier that there were some wounded soldiers that needed to be treated. Among them, she was told, one was a Russian soldier, captured during one of the recent battles on the outskirts of Mykolaiv. The idea of needing to treat an enemy soldier was making her nauseated.

As she walked through the hospital halls, she noticed that the number of people being treated was increasing each day at an alarming rate. There were so many wounded! And not just soldiers, but civilians! Women, older people, kids. Some of them sustained injuries worse than anything she'd ever seen. There were even several dead bodies inside body bags just lying in the corridors. Evidently there must have been so many dead that there was no more space where to place the corpses. It was unsettling.

After a few minutes she reached the ward where she'd be working. A couple of other nurses were already there, tending to the wounded. The Russian soldier was in a separate room on his own. He was laying on a hospital bed, his head turned towards the window. His left leg was bandaged in several places.

When Solomiya entered the room, the soldier heard her and turned his head to look in her direction. He was incredibly young, slightly older than a teenager. This was unmistakable, even despite scrapes and bruises on his face.

"Hello," he said mildly.

Solomiya ignored his greeting and her face was still stern. Anger was boiling up inside of her. This man, this being, this creature, he was part of the enemy's forces, the same forces that brought death and destruction with them, the same ones that killed Tymur, the same ones that were going to continue to kill many more people. And yet, she was supposed to help them? To waste her time and precious medical resources on this monster. A part of her wanted to grab a scalpel or another surgical tool and just jam it in his throat, to make him feel the pain that she was going through. But this wasn't going to change anything. This would not stop the pain being inflicted on countless civilians and this would not bring her beloved back from the dead.

"I know you probably feel hatred towards me," the soldier continued after a minute of silence.

"Hatred? If only that was accurate enough to describe what I'm feeling," Solomiya replied in an ice-cold tone of voice.

"I am sorry. I had no say in any of this."

"You carried out the orders – to kill, to destroy, to inflict pain."

"I didn't do any of that. I've not shot anyone. I was delivering supplies to the others."

Solomiya didn't respond and instead picked up the medical report left by another nurse which detailed the wounds this soldier sustained. Solomiya began scanning through it.

The soldier's name – Pavel Morozov, age 19. Three bullet wounds in the left leg, two in the thigh and one in the calf, all were flesh wounds and did not damage the bones. He lost a fair amount of blood, however, and there were signs of infection.

"They say I'll be alright soon," Pavel spoke again.

"You could say you're lucky. No shattered bones and no major arteries damaged. But you'll need to stay here for at least a few more days. You'll be feeling feverish and weak."

"I understand everything. I'll stay for as long as needed. Will it just be you looking after me today?"

"No, the other nurses will be around too. Somebody will keep checking on your condition regularly."

"Thank you, nurse."

Solomiya did not respond afterwards and instead began preparing the medication that would need to be administered to stop the infection spreading at the soldier's wounds. In her head, she was constantly fighting with herself. *"Why should I bother to save this man?"* was a recurring thought. Each time, however, she kept bringing herself back that her duty was to save lives regardless of who the people were, that fighting evil with more evil was not a solution.

Her thought process was interrupted by a loud, thunderous clamour coming from outside. More shelling. It lasted for almost a minute while she stood still. A few of the impacts sounded very close. Too close. Solomiya still couldn't get used to such a terrifying sound. She knew that whenever it came, it meant only one thing – more death. She imagined what would happen if this very hospital was hit. The doctors and the nurses couldn't exactly spend the entire time in the underground shelters. They needed to work round the clock, and in recent days the number of injured people coming into the hospital only increased. They simply had to continue working and saving lives regardless of what was going on outside.

"You know, I didn't realise at first what we were doing," Pavel said once the shelling stopped. "We were told we would be fighting extremists, not peaceful civilians."

Solomiya looked in his direction, feeling lost and not knowing how to even respond to that. After failing to pick her words, she just sighed. Pavel continued:

"Don't worry. You don't need to respond to me. I'm just thinking out loud. I'm having a hard time reconciling what I've been told by my superiors and what I've been seeing here over the last few days."

"I'm afraid at this point in time, it's too late," Solomiya interjected. "Many good people have died already, including the love of my life."

"I am sorry to hear that."

Solomiya didn't want to talk about it anymore and his sorry was meaningless to her. It was too painful to discuss this. She finished administering the medicine and then silently walked out of the room to tend to other wounded.

Once she was back in the corridor, she saw Nadiya there too, approaching closer. Nadiya smiled when she saw Solomiya and gave her a hug.

"Solomiya, glad to see you're fighting on. How's today?"

"Today is the same as yesterday. Just a continuous struggle with my thoughts and emotions."

"It will get better, dear. Trust me on this."

"I know. I just hope it will be soon. I don't know how much longer I can fight myself."

"Don't try to suppress your pain. You need to let it out. Only then you can move forward."

"I understand. Thanks, Nadiya."

"As always. By the way, today is my last day for a while. I'll be going to Kropyvnytskyi tomorrow where my parents live," Nadiya reminded her.

"Of course. I hope there will be less craziness over there than here. You deserve a little break."

"Oh, I'll be working there too. I'm afraid no breaks for us. People need medical care everywhere at this time."

They agreed to stay in contact and said goodbyes to each other. Nadiya carried on along the corridor to the next ward, whilst Solomiya resumed her work here. She still needed to check on other wounded and lots of work was ahead. Time did not wait for her pain to heal and people depended on her. She knew that well and she knew she had to stay strong.

A loud noise from outside alerted Maria while she was peacefully sitting and playing a little word game with her daughter Alina. Her husband Artur was sleeping at the time as he got very little sleep the night before due to air raid alarms. The noise that was coming from outside awoke him. It wasn't a noise of missiles raining down on the buildings. It was something else.

"Alina, stay here and keep your head down," Maria told her daughter and then got up really fast and ran towards one of the windows.

Artur joined her and looked out of another window. At first it wasn't clear where the noise was coming from, but after a few more seconds they finally saw what was causing it. A big line of tanks entered their neighbourhood. These were enemy tanks as they were clearly marked with a letter 'Z' - a strange symbol that the invaders had on a lot of their military vehicles. Some of the tanks forcefully knocked down the wooden fences of nearby houses and parked in their back gardens, the others continued further.

A sharp, cold sensation of fear overtook Maria. The occupiers had passed through this area before, although it was only briefly and in smaller numbers. Now, however, a whole group of them came here and it looked like they were aiming to stay.

Russian soldiers were now walking all over the street in front, some were approaching the front doors of people's homes and knocking. Two of the soldiers approached their house. The cold sensation Maria was feeling increased its intensity and she started getting a cold sweat all over. *Why are they coming here? What do they want?*

The soldiers were now at their front door, knocking. Artur walked slowly up to the door, reluctant to open it. It was, however, no use trying to pretend that they were not home. That wouldn't have stopped the soldiers, who might've even attempted to break in. Artur decided to open the door.

"Yes?" he asked.

"We need everyone out of the houses and onto the street," one of the soldiers demanded.

"Why? What's going on?"

"Shut up and do as you're told! Is it just you two?"

One of the soldiers looked inside their house and appeared to have seen Alina in the living room.

"You too. Over here," he signalled for Alina to come over.

Maria was frozen in terror and desperately wanted to know what these soldiers were planning to do. As Alina came up to the front door, Maria grabbed her by the hand and brought her closer to herself. She would not let anyone hurt her daughter.

"Bring your phones with you, and if you have any tablets or laptops, bring them too," the Russian soldier continued making his demands.

"Ok," Artur obeyed and took his phone out.

Maria followed suit and took hers out too.

"Just these?" the soldier asked, expecting them to surrender their other gadgets too.

"Yes," Artur said firmly.

The soldiers then motioned for them to exit the house and follow them. The other soldiers were doing the same to other residents of the area, getting them all onto the street and putting them into groups.

"Artur, what are they doing?" Maria whispered to her husband.

"I don't know. Maybe they want to loot our homes," he guessed.

Maria felt like the nightmare of this invasion was about to get worse. The feeling inside her kept ringing an alarm at full intensity, telling her to run as fast as she could, but she couldn't leave her family and her home behind.

The enemy soldiers then began to separate the men from the women and children. One of the men tried to resist being separated from two of his small children, so the soldiers knocked him onto the ground and began violently stomping on him in an attempt to teach him and everyone else a lesson. Artur was taken from Maria and Alina too and pushed into a group with other men.

"You five, form a line over there," one of the soldiers pointed at the group Artur was in. Another soldier took a few other men with him.

"Can we please discuss this peacefully?" Artur tried to reason with one of the soldiers. "We're just civilians. We're not armed at all."

The soldier ignored him completely and instructed for them all to get on their knees. Artur and the other men in his group did as they were told, hoping not to anger the occupiers. The Russian soldier walked up to the first of the men and took that man's phone from his hands in order to look at the messages on it.

"Have you been sending any messages to the Ukrainian Armed Forces? Huh?" the soldier yelled right in the man's face.

"No, of course not."

"Good."

He kept the man's phone and then walked over to the next man, forcefully taking a phone from his hand too.

"And you? Colluding with Ukrainian officials, are you?"

"No."

"I don't believe you."

"It's the truth. What do you want me to say?"

The soldier raised his gun and aimed at the man. Maria's heart began racing and pounding like a frantic drum. *Would they really shoot him just like that?*

The Russian soldier continued aiming his assault rifle at the civilian's head, and then at the last moment he lifted his rifle up slightly and shot just over the man's head. Every civilian in the area jumped from shock and fear.

"Perhaps I'll believe you for now," the soldier said and then continued further.

He now walked up to Artur and snatched his phone as well.

"So, are you a spy? Huh? Been posting any anti-Russian messages?"

"No. I've just been at home, trying to keep my family safe," Artur responded in as calm tone of voice as he could.

"Lies! You work for the Ukrainian military."

The enemy soldier then aimed his rifle at Artur and without any delay shot at him. Maria screamed at the moment this occurred, terror taking over her within a fraction of a second, ripping all the air out of her lungs and making her choke. As Artur collapsed onto the ground with a bullet hole in his head and a puddle of blood forming on the ground, Maria fell on her knees, crying and grasping her daughter tightly. A flood of violently painful emotions filled her. A sense of hopelessness took over that was flowing into anger and depression at the same time.

Alina was sobbing together with her mother. She was holding onto Maria at the neck and pressing her face against her mother's cheek. For a moment Maria wanted to recklessly attack the Russian soldier just so that she'd die right there and join her husband, but knowing her daughter was still there, she couldn't do such a thing. She knew Alina needed her and she could not abandon her.

The soldier who shot Artur then walked up to two other men who were on their knees. They were trembling whilst holding their phones up. The soldier took their phones and didn't even look through them.

"I'm going to give the two of you a chance," he said. "You see the road ahead? You can make a run for it. Go to your freedom, if you wish."

The two men remained as they were, confused by what he just said to them.

"Are you deaf? Go on then, get up! Run if you can! If you don't move in three seconds, I'm going to shoot you."

Both men quickly got up onto their feet and in a panic began backing away. The Russian soldier laughed and started firing his gun at the ground next to their feet. The two civilian men got terrified even more and broke into a full run. The Russian soldier then aimed higher and fired at both fleeing men, taking both down with ease, as though it was just casual target practice for him.

"Khokhli never learn," he said to himself and then headed to join other soldiers.

Maria was in utter shock and horror at what she was witnessing. She was seeing pure cruelty unfold in front of her eyes and in front of the eyes of her daughter. She couldn't stop her tears at all. All she could think about was why they were punished so harshly and inhumanely. As she gazed around, she saw other Russian soldiers carrying out similar acts of cruelty on other civilian men – executing them on their knees, or making them run, only to get shot in the back, or simply beating them to a pulp. She could not even imagine that human beings could be so sadistic, to just kill civilians for fun. She realised that pure evil arrived in Bucha that day.

Chapter 5

8th of March
Mariupol

Danyil and Lera were waiting in a big crowd of people. Another green corridor was about to be opened to allow Mariupol civilians to escape the war zone. A 'green corridor' was an official term used to mean a safe, demilitarised passageway through which civilians could escape dangerous areas during a war. In the last few days, two such corridors were established in Mariupol, but they quickly collapsed due to unexpected shelling, and the evacuations failed.

This time round Danyil hoped the evacuation would work. He knew that he and his sister had to try escaping. It was hopeless to stay in a city that was gradually edging closer to its inevitable doom. Their parents had gone missing and were probably dead, their apartment was destroyed, the invaders kept getting closer, and the city's basic services were continuing to fail. In the last few days, there had been frequent power cuts because of shelling, with no electricity for days, and clean water was also hard to come by. Food in the supermarkets was running low and the canned supplies weren't enough for everyone. If they didn't leave now, things would only get worse.

The people in the crowd were very anxious. They wanted to get out of this place as soon as possible, but many were doubtful if that would ever happen. There were a few buses waiting at the bus stop already and the queue of civilians towards them was growing by the minute.

"I get a feeling that we'll be stuck here for good," said Lera to her brother all of a sudden.

"Don't think like that. We'll find a way," Danyil refused to surrender himself to the situation.

"It is not up to us and you know it."

"Would you rather that we don't try?"

"No, that's not what I said. I just don't believe in hope anymore," Lera's words were very glum.

Danyil could understand what she was feeling. To a large degree, he felt the same way, but something deep inside of him refused to give up. He was a fighter and he was going to do everything possible to get himself and his sister to safety. He knew that they had to survive this no matter what.

Someone ahead gave a signal and buses opened their doors. Civilians at the front of the queue began boarding them. Seemed that the green corridor had finally been opened.

"Please don't let anything bad to happen this time," Danyil murmured quietly to himself.

A minute went by and everything was fine. Two minutes. Three. And then he heard sounds of bombardment nearby. He and all the other civilians looked in the direction of the sound but could see nothing. *Did that happen somewhere far away? Was the bus stop still safe?*

As if by speak of a devil, a screeching sound of a missile was then heard and half a second later the bus stop was hit with a thunderous cacophony. Fire broke out and debris flew everywhere. Two buses were completely ablaze with civilians running out of them in a hurry. Huge clouds of black smoke were coming from the bus stop. The crowd began scattering away quickly. Danyil grabbed his sister by the hand and followed suit. It was no longer safe staying there. It was never really safe there to begin with. All these promises of green corridors were all lies. Danyil felt angry with himself for even hoping that all this could work out. The first two times the civilian evacuations failed should've been a sign.

They both ran as fast as their feet could manage whilst simultaneously carrying small suitcases with their possessions. Lera almost tripped up, but Danyil held her hand tighter and stopped her fall. As they ran behind a nearby building, they stopped to catch their breath.

"Lera, did you get hurt?"

"No, no, I am fine. Just give me a moment."

They were both in shock. Even despite the expectation that things would most likely go wrong, the shelling they just witnessed still shook them to the very core. This was the closest they had been to a missile hit and it was beyond terrifying. Danyil's ears were still ringing and he could still hear the echoes of civilian screams, unsure if they were actually happening somewhere at the distance or if he was imagining it. He didn't know what to feel at this moment – anger, fear, depression. All those feelings were there, competing with each other for dominance but ultimately ending up merging together into something unexplainable.

"What are our options now?" Lera asked.

"I honestly don't know. We must return to the shelter for now."

"I told you we'll never get out of here. We're cursed to stay here."

"No. There is a way out. And if there isn't, we'll come up with one. I won't give up, Lera," Danyil told her whilst channelling his inner anger into determination.

Once the two of them caught their breath, they continued running, hoping to make it back to the shelter without coming under any more shelling.

9th of March
Bucha

The past four days Maria did not want to do anything. She was just laying on a makeshift bed in the shelter, grieving the loss of her husband and wishing she could turn back the time and escape this place before the invaders came. During the nights, she was holding Alina very tightly out of fear of losing her dear daughter too.

They had to sleep in the same bed as the space in the shelter was very limited and several other people were there with them too. The Russian soldiers kicked them all out of their homes and forced them to stay in crowded shelters, dark cellars and dirty barns, whilst the soldiers themselves occupied the homes of their captives.

Finally Maria got tired of fighting her own thoughts and decided to distract herself. She looked around frantically for her daughter and saw Alina sitting on a blanket on the floor and reading a children's book. She breathed a sigh of relief and consoled herself. Every person in the shelter was busy, quietly minding their own business. She decided to join her daughter on the blanket and to see what she was reading.

"Alina, how are you feeling?"

"I'm ok, mum."

"Are you sure? Because you can tell me anything."

"I'm really sad and I want those soldiers to leave."

"Me too, darling. We all want them to leave. And soon our own soldiers will come and will throw them out."

Alina seemed to have understood and continued reading her book. Maria decided to let her whilst sitting in silence next to her. The silence lasted for a few more minutes until it was interrupted by booming noises outside. Everyone in the shelter got alerted. It did not sound like falling missiles. It sounded like cannon fire. Perhaps a battle was going on?

Among the people hiding in the shelter, two of the younger guys headed up to the entrance to see what all the noise was about. One of the women in the shelter also went after them. Everybody was curious. Maria decided to check as well as she had nothing else to do. She checked on Alina again to be sure her daughter was all right and then got off the blanket on the floor and went towards the shelter entrance too.

"What's happening out there?" Maria asked the others who were looking out onto the street from the shelter.

"They're shooting at something," one of the men replied and continued looking.

Maria crept a bit closer to the exit. The two guys stepped outside, so Maria did too, inspecting the area ahead where the noises were coming from. A moment later Maria spotted one of the tanks moving along the road and stopping. It got into position and then fired with its cannon, causing more deafening noises.

"They're shooting at the parked cars on the street," one of the men then said.

"What for?" Maria asked.

"Some kind of sick entertainment for them."

Maria did not want to stay there any longer. She just turned back and walked inside the shelter. She felt like she and her daughter were stuck in this hell for a while, needing to put up with cruelty, humiliation and destructive behaviour of the occupiers until somebody taught them a lesson.

10th of March
Kyiv

Kyiv city was fortifying itself for days whilst it continued getting besieged by the Russian army. Although the enemies were repelled, they remained around 30 kilometres from the city and were attempting to encircle it. Many volunteers were helping to get the city prepared in case the worst came to worst and the enemies got inside. Oleksiy was among them. Over the last week he and Dmytro kept joining many others who were setting up barricades all over the city, covering historical monuments to prevent them getting destroyed, digging trenches and helping to set up hedgehogs on the roads. Hedgehogs were sturdy metallic barricades that consisted of three steel beams welded together across each other. They were useful in impeding the tanks in case any enemy tanks managed to get into the city streets.

"I'm drained," Oleksiy said after he placed yet another sandbag onto a barricade and sat down on it. He could feel himself sweating underneath his warm jumper.

"You need a break. You've been here since the early morning," Dmytro noted.

"Well, every minute each of us gives is crucial. What if the enemy gets inside the city tomorrow? We need to be ready for any scenario."

"Yeah, I understand you, brother."

"By the way, I'm going to be helping to deliver some supplies over the next few days to places on the outskirts of the city. Defenders and civilians in those areas need regular deliveries. Would you be willing to come as well?"

"Of course. It will be a bit more engaging than just digging trenches non-stop."

A few distant sounds of bombardment were heard. Oleksiy and Dmytro stopped their conversation and looked in the direction of where they heard the sound coming from. Even though it was distant and they couldn't even see anything, it was scary and kept everyone on alert. They needed to be ready to flee into cover at a very short notice in case bombardments got closer.

"All right, I better resume the work," Oleksiy got back up onto his feet when his phone suddenly rang.

Dmytro shook his head and laughed as Oleksiy sat back down and took his phone out of the pocket. His mum was calling him. He answered the call.

"How's it going, mum?"

"Oleksiy! It is great to hear your voice. How are you managing everything? You've not called for two days and I've been starting to get worried."

"Just been busy helping to set up city defences. And when coming back home, I've been so exhausted that I've been falling asleep right away."

"I see. Please be careful and watch yourself. They are firing many missiles towards Kyiv."

"I know, mum. I'll try my best to stay safe. How's Diana doing?"

"She's doing her university studies through online right now. She wants to do well in the year end exams."

"That's great. I'm glad she's able to continue her studies despite the war. Send my best wishes to her."

His mother then told him that both she and Diana missed him very much and wanted for him to call them more regularly. Oleksiy knew perfectly well that his mother was worried sick for him and his wellbeing, so he promised to call them both as regularly as possible. He didn't want his family to worry. The whole situation was distressing enough already and he only wanted to make it easier for his loved ones.

When the call ended, he stood still for a bit, gazing at the ground and just thinking of how life was like just mere weeks ago, before the invasion started. Despite some difficulties in making ends meet and paying the bills, life was good before. There was peace and security, and loved ones were nearby. And now everything was chaotic and unpredictable. There was no guarantee that tomorrow would come, and it was not possible to plan anything for the foreseeable future. Every day had to be survived through separately, one at a time.

10th of March
Somewhere near Kherson

Taras lost track of the time of the day it was now. He along with 24 other prisoners were kept in a tiny room for many hours of the day. It was so cramped in there that some of them had to sleep standing up or to be pressed into a corner in an awkward position. It was stuffy in the room. There was very little ventilation there - only a small gap between the only door and the floor, and a tiny grate on one of the walls. Breathing already proved to be a great challenge, yet alone talking or moving. Taras understood perfectly that their captors were trying everything to humiliate them. They could've chosen to keep them in any other room in the building that was bigger and better ventilated, but they deliberately picked the smallest one. They picked a room that was used as storage rather than one used as living quarters.

At the very least they were not in total darkness, he thought to himself. At least there was just enough light to faintly see the faces of other prisoners and to look around the room.

"You also can't sleep?" a voice came from Taras' right-hand side.

He turned his head slightly, as much as he could. A prisoner that was next to him was awake.

"I barely slept at all since they brought us here," Taras admitted.

"Me too. Each time I start to fall asleep, I keep thinking that I may not wake up from it."

Taras just shrugged his big shoulders and turned his head back to face downward.

"My name is Roman, by the way," the other prisoner continued. "I was stationed in the South of Kherson when all this started. And you?"

"Taras."

"Which unit are you in?"

"I'm actually a police officer."

"Oh, understood. But you too were helping to defend the city when it was captured, right?"

"That's right," Taras confirmed. Talking was starting to tire him out. He tried taking a deep breath in, but all he felt was musty air full of sweat and body odour.

"I hope your family is safe at least," Roman continued after a brief pause.

"They are out of the country already."

"Mine too. Figured it was better to be safe than sorry."

A few minutes later there were footsteps outside the room. Someone was coming. There was a sound of the door unlocking before it swung open and bright lights streamed into the room, flooding every corner of it. Because it was so dim in the room before, having the light come on so suddenly hurt Taras' eyes and he had to close them for a moment and allow them to adjust gradually.

Two Russian soldiers were at the door, both holding guns.

"Recreation time. You all may watch TV in the hall for the next hour," said one of the soldiers and stepped back out of the room.

The prisoners began moving in a slow and sluggish fashion, feeling sore and dizzy, but being pleased that they could finally get out of this suffocating room and stretch their feet a bit. Taras and Roman were among the last ones to exit.

The main hall was a lot larger than the room they were kept in normally, and was pretty spacious, so all the prisoners could sit and move around the hall without it feeling cramped. There were a few barred windows in the hall, through which light could come in, but they were high up along the wall. All the doors leading out of the main hall were either locked or guarded. A small, flat-screen TV was placed against one of the walls in the hall. It was showing one of the Russian channels. Taras didn't bother to pay attention to what was on as it looked a lot like some political propaganda.

"I swear the time stands still when we're in that tiny room," Roman stopped by Taras' side.

"Well, don't expect them to make our life easy outside of it either," Taras responded. "They will make us appreciate the time spent inside that room."

"What do you mean?"

"Look over there."

Taras pointed with his gaze alone towards a small group of Russian soldiers. They were fiercely discussing something and approaching their direction where most of the prisoners were. Taras could sense that some act of cruelty and humiliation was about to come from these soldiers.

When the soldiers were close enough and within earshot of all the prisoners, they stopped and readied their assault rifles.

"Your attention, please!" one of the soldiers raised the tone of his voice.

Every prisoner stopped what he was doing and turned to face their captors.

"Gather around over here and form a line. Quickly!"

The prisoners did as they were told. Many were starting to feel anxious and it was showing up clearly on their faces.

"We're all going to have a little lesson of loyalty," the soldier continued. "I want every single one of you on my command to say 'Glory to Russia'. Say it like you mean it, clear?"

"Here it comes," thought Taras. The next phase of their humiliation tactics and mental torture was about to come. They could force you to say or do anything they wanted, and if you disobeyed, they hurt you.

"So, let us begin," the Russian soldier continued, "on my command!"

He lifted his left hand up in an open palm to gesture for everyone to do as he commanded. Most prisoners feebly mumbled 'Glory to Russia' without putting any effort into it.

"What the hell was that!?" the Russian soldier exploded in a fit of anger. "You call that following my command!? Again!"

He did the same gesture as before. The prisoners raised their voices a bit when repeating the phrase, but they still sounded feeble and unmotivated. One of the Russian soldiers took a few steps forward, walking right up to one of the prisoners so that their faces were only a few centimetres apart.

"You! Say 'Glory to Russia' now!" the soldier demanded.

"Go to hell!" the prisoner disobeyed with a bitter defiance.

Another Russian soldier who was behind the prisoner pushed the prisoner forward. As the man stumbled forward, the Russian soldier in front of him struck him in the face with the butt of the rifle, knocking him onto the ground. Before the prisoner could get back to his senses, both Russian soldiers began kicking him hard and stomping on his ankles. It was hard to watch, but Taras knew he would have to get used to it. Not only would this become a daily occurrence, but eventually he too would be on the receiving end of it.

When the kicking of the poor prisoner stopped, one of the Russian soldiers continued walking along the line that the other prisoners formed, looking each one in the eyes. He then randomly pointed at one of them.

"Your turn. Say that you love Russia."

The prisoner said what he was asked to say but in a defeated and highly reluctant tone of voice. The Russian soldier elbowed him in the face hard and split his lower lip.

"Better, but still pathetic," he said and continued walking and gazing every prisoner in the eyes.

He paused for a moment when he reached Taras. He was noticeably shorter than Taras but continued trying to intimidate Taras with his fierce gaze. A moment later he struck Taras with the butt of the rifle in the ribs. Taras felt a sharp influx of pain and clutched the spot where he was hit, trying hard to suppress any grunts.

"I don't like how you're looking at me, you filthy scum!" the Russian soldier said to him. "You better watch your body language."

Finally the soldier walked back a few steps to where other soldiers were standing. A few seconds of intense silence followed before he turned to the prisoners again.

"We'll keep doing this every day until I hear you all admit loud and clear how much you love Russia. We'll beat that Ukrainian defiance out of you. For now get back to your activities. You have 45 minutes of free time left."

The ruscist soldiers turned around and headed for the other end of the main hall, leaving the prisoners free to do what they wanted for some more time. The man who was beaten up was still on the ground, holding onto one of his knees that was kicked hard. A couple of other prisoners walked over to him to help him up. The others dispersed slowly, simultaneously feeling an uncontrollable rage and a crushing despair.

"You all right?" Roman asked Taras.

"Yeah. That was to be expected."

"Fucking orcs only like the language of violence. Nothing good ever comes from them."

"We'll need to be strong if we want to endure their attempts at humiliating us. And we need to stick together as a whole group. When the time comes, these orcs will get what's coming to them."

Taras said that last sentence with a hint of anger and determination in his voice. He was sure he would make the Russian soldiers pay for everything. He just needed to think on how to do it.

11th of March
Mykolaiv

Solomiya was about to finish her shift for the day. It was a long and tiring shift, like any other over the past two weeks. Her mental state continued to be fragile, although the initial wave of hopelessness had subsided. Now there was just a numb and aimless feeling of limbo that dominated her mind.

As she walked down a corridor, preparing to leave the hospital, a senior nurse, Vira, came up to her.

"Solomiya, before you go, can you come here for a minute?"

Solomiya agreed and followed the nurse. Unexpected situations were common these days, so Solomiya was expecting that perhaps her help was still needed. She was exhausted both mentally and physically, but she was always prepared to help other people, especially if their lives depended on it.

Vira led her into a nearby ward. As they entered, in a hospital bed directly in front of the door Solomiya saw a little girl. The girl was unconscious, with a life support machine attached to her. Upon a closer look, Solomiya saw that the girl's left arm was gone and there was just a bandaged up stomp in its place. Seeing the little girl in such terrible state, Solomiya's heart began pounding hard.

"What happened to her?" she asked, her voice quiet almost like a whisper, and a small tear was now coming down her face.

"This is Zlata. She is 10 years old. There were some cluster bomb attacks in the city these days," the senior nurse replied, "Our enemies are relentless and cruel as you see."

Solomiya heard about the cluster bombs. These were bombs that upon exploding released smaller bombs that would pepper a small area with more explosions. Such weapons were banned for use on civilian areas, but it was obvious by now that the enemy did not care for civilian casualties and was deliberately conducting such acts of terror. Vira then continued:

"When it hit the apartment building, a few of the smaller bombs got into this girl's apartment and destroyed it. Both of her parents died instantly while trying to protect her. She's lucky to be alive and to only lose one arm."

"Will she make it?"

"I don't know. She is stable for now. We'll do everything we can to save her, but anything can happen down the line. I'll need a few of our nurses to be checking up on her regularly and being here to monitor her condition. Would you be up for this in your next few shifts?"

"Absolutely," Solomiya agreed without even a thought. She felt very strongly for this little girl and wanted to do everything possible to save her life. "I'll be here every day if I have to."

"Thanks, Solomiya. I knew coming to you was the right decision. You were always great with the kids. Now there's one other thing regarding her."

"I'm listening."

"We've checked all the records and it appears she doesn't have any family left. All grandparents are dead and neither mother nor father had any siblings. She's an orphan now. And perhaps the hardest thing is having to tell her that her parents are gone if she pulls through and wakes up."

"We'll think of something. The main task right now is to make sure she recovers," Solomiya said and Vira seemed to be in agreement with that.

"All right, Solomiya. She'll be in your care then during your upcoming shifts. Go and get some rest now. You really deserved it. You've been working yourself to the ground these few days."

Solomiya exited the ward and back into the corridor. She couldn't get Zlata's physical state out of her mind. The poor little girl's life was hanging by the threads and all her family was now gone and she had no-one.

Once back in the corridor, Solomiya saw Pavel, the captive Russian soldier whom she treated a few times over the last few days. A couple of nurses were with him, filling in some forms.

"Hello," Pavel greeted her. "Thank you for everything you've done for me. I'm being discharged now."

Solomiya warmed up to Pavel a bit, despite the feelings of bitterness and hatred she held towards the enemy army. Pavel seemed to have been repentant and understanding about the horrible things his country was doing.

"Glad you're better now," Solomiya acknowledged. "Where will you be taken now?"

"A camp for prisoners of war. I'll be doing some manual labour work there."

"Tough days ahead then, just like for the rest of us."

"I'll manage it," Pavel was full of purpose. "If helping your people through manual labour is what I need to do to atone for my sins, then I'll do it."

"Thank you, Pavel. I wish all the Russian soldiers thought the same way. Best of luck to you there."

"And to you."

Solomiya grabbed her belongings and left the hospital a few minutes later. It was evening time already and the sun was setting. A lot of thoughts were racing through her head. Most of all, she couldn't get Zlata out of her head. She felt some kind of connection to that little girl, that she needed to protect her.

On the way home, she decided to take a small detour and walk through the city streets a bit. She needed to have some time to put her thoughts in order. Everything in her head was in chaos and she felt that her life came to a standstill and got turned inside out. She began asking herself if there was a purpose in continuing living or if this was the end, whether it was just easier to abandon this world and not experience any more pain that it had to bring. However, she also knew this was merely the darkness within her talking and that she just needed some more time to let herself heal. She was good at healing others, but she had no idea how she could heal herself.

She stopped and glanced at one of the buildings that sustained damage from shelling. That building was not just a building. It was someone's home, an important part of someone's life. And now whoever lived there likely had nowhere else to go.

She continued on, still thinking about everything and trying to make sense of it in her head. *What if this war goes on for months or even longer?* Horror overtook her when she considered a possibility that the war could go on for a long time, bringing with it more deaths of innocent people, more destruction of cities, and more grief. And worst of all, there was nothing she personally could do about it. She always believed that when there were problems in her life, she was always within power to make changes and fix those problems. But what could she do about a war? What could she do about Tymur's death? These events were beyond her control and she was absolutely powerless to change them.

She sat down on a bench in a park, still thinking, deciding on her future, if there even was one. Living each day as though it was her last – this kind of existence was not sustainable. She took out a small photo that she always carried with herself, a photo of her with Tymur. They looked so happy together there. Seeing it triggered a powerful flow of emotions and she began to cry. She couldn't stop this surge of emotions. She just needed to let them all out.

An old man was walking by at that moment, noticing Solomiya sitting on a park bench and crying.

"Are you ok, dear?" he asked.

"Just thinking about my life," she replied and lifted her head. "I don't know what to do with it. I feel powerless."

"Choices, or lack thereof. I understand. Sometimes we feel that we can't change the course of events," he reasoned, "and it's true. You and I cannot stop what is happening to our country. But you can take care of yourself and those around you. You can make their lives better."

"I failed to save the man I loved. And now I'm afraid to bring anyone else closer to my life, because what if they will die too?"

"And if you don't, you'll always be in pain. You can't go on through life by yourself. If we only live our lives just for ourselves, then why do we live? What purpose is there in that? The people we bring close to our heart, they make our life worth living. Remember that."

On that note the old man continued on his way. Solomiya remained staring into distance, mulling over what the old man just said. And perhaps he was right. Perhaps closing in on herself and dwelling in her head all the time whilst keeping others at arm's length was too self-destructive. *Losing someone you love is always scary. But refusing to love anyone out of fear of losing them, that is even worse.*

12th of March
Bucha

Every day in the shelter was the same as the last. Maria kept hoping that something would change and the cruel invaders that had killed so many innocent Ukrainians would be driven out. But nothing was changing. The guilty continued to commit horrifying deeds and nobody was doing anything about it. Nobody was punishing them for what they were doing. How could there be any justice in the world if the most evil men went unpunished?

Footsteps came from the entrance of the shelter. Everyone inside got quiet, waiting in trepidation, not having any clue of what was coming, but knowing full well that it could not be anything good. Two young Russian soldiers emerged from the corridor and into the room, not saying anything, and instead just scanning everyone. There was a deathly silence in the room for a few seconds.

"You," one of them pointed at Maria, "over here."

Maria froze in terror. She couldn't move. Her heart was racing.

"Are you deaf? Come over here right now."

Maria released her daughter and began slowly edging her feet one by one towards the soldiers.

"Your daughter as well," the other soldier spoke in a demanding tone.

Anxiety was running amok in Maria's stomach. She was terrified already at what the soldiers would do to her, but now imagining a possibility they could hurt Alina too was just too unbearable.

"Please let her stay here," Maria pleaded.

"She is coming too. Now!" demanded one of the soldiers while lifting his rifle up.

Maria turned to her daughter, catching her gaze, and nodded for her to follow. The two of them slowly stepped forward till they were a meter from the soldiers. The soldiers turned around and proceeded to exit the shelter; Maria and Alina followed them, tightly holding hands so not to lose one another.

It got dark outside already. The day was ending and it was getting very cold. Maria was shivering, but she wasn't sure if she was shivering because of the cold or because she was utterly terrified of what the soldiers were about to do to them. She began playing all sorts of scenarios in her head, wondering what was to come. They're going to interrogate and torture her, she thought, or worse, torture her daughter in front of her. And then they were going to shoot them both. Was there still a chance to make a run for it? No. The two soldiers were armed with assault rifles. She'd never make it a few meters without getting shot, especially if she had to carry Alina in her arms too.

They passed a couple of other soldiers who were absolutely drunk out of their wits and laughing like maniacs at some sick joke. One of them threw a glass bottle really hard at a wall of a nearby house, shattering it and then continuing his silly laughter. None of this was making Maria feel easier. On the contrary, it only kept fuelling her fears.

The soldiers that were leading them finally stopped at the main entrance door to one of the houses. They entered and motioned for Maria and Alina to go in as well. There was no-one else in the house. *"Yeah, they are going to kill us,"* thought Maria. She hesitantly turned towards the outside whilst standing in the doorway, but then realised that it was too late to exit the house. One of the soldiers shut the door and began aggressively shoving Maria into the room.

"Now take your clothes off, dear," the more hideous of the two soldiers said whilst grinning.

"I..." Maria hesitated.

The other soldier grabbed Alina by the shoulder and pointed a gun to her head.

"Do as he says or your daughter gets it."

Maria wanted to fall to the ground and cry here, but she knew she had to be strong. She couldn't endanger Alina's life. She couldn't allow them to hurt her. Quietly but with great vacillation she unbuttoned her jacket and took it off. She was doing it all slowly, trying to stall time, as though hoping that something would change in the few seconds she was adding to each action.

"Go on," the hideous-looking soldier pointed at her top so that it could come off next.

With trembling hands Maria grabbed onto her top and began slowly taking it off. An ice-cold lump was churning in her stomach. The hideous soldier stepped closer to her once her top was off, gazing her up and down, his breath stinking of alcohol. He reached his hand forward to touch Maria, but she instinctively pulled back and slapped his hand out of the way. That appeared to have enraged the soldier.

"Right, I will not have this kind of behaviour here!" he yelled. "Kneel down right now!"

Maria did as he told, hoping not to anger him anymore.

"Put your hands on the floor! Do it!"

Hesitantly she put her hands on the wooden floor.

A sharp pain suddenly jolted all over her body and she screamed before even realising what happened. The fingers of her right hand were burning from pain beneath the Russian soldier's boot. When he took the boot off her hand, she pulled it back and grabbed onto it, screaming in agony and unable to open her eyes. It seemed as though all sensation was lost from her fingers whilst simultaneously they were throbbing from immense pain. She could hear Alina weeping and her heart sank even more.

When Maria finally managed to stop screaming and opened her eyes, the hideous soldier grabbed her other hand and sharply twisted her wrist. She could hear bones crunching and a jolt of pain now in the other hand too.

"Stop! Please!" she begged.

"Will you be a good girl then?" the soldier asked while bringing his face down to her level.

Maria didn't say anything. She couldn't. She was still groaning from pain.

"I'll take that as a yes. Now, get up."

Maria obeyed whilst avoiding eye contact with that monster of a human being. He set his gun down and then grabbed her by the shoulders on both sides.

"Hurry up, Pasternak! I want to have a go at that big-titted beauty too," the other soldier spoke from the other end of the room whilst still holding Alina firmly.

"Shut up, Sokolov! You'll get your turn."

He then crudely pushed Maria onto the armchair that was behind her, causing her to lose her balance and fall onto it. Maria knew she could not fight back or else they would hurt Alina, but she continued feeling weak and helpless, not knowing how she would endure being raped by two repulsive human beings and right in front of her daughter.

Pasternak leaned down closer to her. The abhorrent stench of his breath was making her sick. She continued avoiding his gaze, looking instead at his feet. His hands were now gliding all over the top part of her body, groping her crudely.

"This will be so enjoyable. I'm going to liberate you, dear," he said, his hands now starting to move down to unbutton Maria's trousers. Maria closed her eyes, her lower jaw was trembling in anticipation of the horrors that were about to come.

All of a sudden a loud gunshot. Her ears rang and she lost her senses for a brief moment. An explosion of blood splashed all over her face. Instinctively her first thought was that they murdered her daughter. She opened her eyes in horror, but instead she saw Pasternak's head covered in blood and him collapsing onto the floor motionlessly. She looked up and saw a man at the entrance. The door was half-open and the man was holding a gun.

"What the hell!?" the other Russian soldier exclaimed whilst turning to face the door.

Momentarily a second gunshot was heard. Maria's heart jumped out of her chest and she froze. A second later the other Russian soldier collapsed onto the ground too. Alina was kneeling down on the floor, holding her ears closed with her hands in fear.

The man at the door did not waste any time. He looked outside briefly and then shut the door and began walking towards Maria. He was an older guy, in his late 50s, and with a messy brown beard.

"Are you all right?" he asked quietly.

"Y-yes," Maria trembled. "Who are you?"

"I'm Georgiy. I knew your husband. Come on, we need to get out of this house before someone catches us."

Maria felt like she could trust him. However, before saying anything else, she got off the armchair and rushed to her daughter.

"Alina, are you hurt?" she asked. "Alina?"

"Mum," Alina was snivelling and was unable to say anything else.

"Alina, dear, we need to go. Hold onto me, ok?"

Alina listened to her mother and tightly grabbed her hand.

"Where are you taking us, Georgiy?" Maria asked as she turned to the older man.

"I live just on the outskirts of town. There are no soldiers there."

"But they are all over the street."

"They won't see us. Just stay close to me."

Georgiy opened the door to the outside and looked out, scanning all directions. Once he established it was clear, he silently motioned to Maria with the gesture of his hand to follow him. They left the house with two dead Russian soldiers and began moving away from it. The two drunk soldiers Maria saw earlier were now passed out on the ground and there were no other soldiers in the immediate vicinity.

Once they walked past the next house, trying to stay in the shadows, Georgiy turned towards the grassy area on the side. Maria and Alina followed and noticed Georgiy jumping down into a trench.

"Come on, this way," he whispered to them.

They did as he advised and joined him in the trench. The trench stretched for quite a distance. It was a reasonably safe place to sneak through as it was harder to be seen when inside it.

"Mind your step," Georgiy said to them whilst stepping over something.

Maria knelt slightly to peer closer and noticed that it was a body bag with a corpse inside. She almost shrieked but held it in, not wishing to alert anyone to their position.

As they walked further, there were more body bags laying in the trench. At one point Maria even had to lift her daughter over a few of them which were stacked on top of one another.

"I'm sorry we have to go through here," Georgiy broke the silence with a quiet murmur. "It's easier to stay concealed this way. I did a lot of the digging here, along with a few other men. The enemy soldiers didn't want to dig this mass grave themselves, so they forced us to do it. And then they made us carry the body bags. They've killed so many innocent people."

"They are savage animals," Maria remarked.

"Worse than that. Savage animals don't do acts of cruelty for fun."

"How did you know where to find us by the way?"

"I've been trying to for a few days now, but I didn't know where they forced you to stay. Then I saw them taking you to that house. I had to wait for the two drunks outside to pass out before I could make my move."

"And where did you get the gun from?"

"That wasn't hard to find. These soldiers have been drinking themselves into unconsciousness every single day. So I snatched a gun from one of them on day one after he passed out."

"And are you sure they won't find us at your place?" Maria was worried and wanted to be sure that she and her daughter would be safe.

"They might, but they rarely go all the way there. They just expect me to come here and do the digging every day and they just leave me alone."

They reached the end of the trench and had to climb back out of it. There were many narrow alleyways and shadowy places ahead, so it was easy to stay out of sight. Georgiy motioned for them to follow him. Maria held her daughter's hand tightly whilst following Georgiy through every part of the location. It was cold and unpleasant, but she would rather be in the cold than in the clutches of those monsters back there, the monsters than held nothing sacred and which lost their humanity long ago.

Chapter 6

16th of March
Mariupol

Conditions in Mariupol were getting worse over the days. Food began getting scarce, water was even scarcer. People had to get water from wells and carry it to their shelters in plastic containers or buckets, and everyone tried to use it very sparingly and only for essential needs such as drinking and cooking. Showers were now a distant dream.

Danyil and Lera were sitting in their shelter, feeling completely beaten by the situation. There was no electricity in the shelter for days and hence no electric lights, no heating, no computers, no way to charge the phones and no way to use any electrical appliances. Because they were eating very little since the invasion began, Danyil noticed that he and his sister got noticeably thinner and lost a lot of weight. His hair was getting scruffier now too as he had no way to get a haircut, and the few items of clothing they were wearing and had with them in the shelter were getting dirty with no way to be washed.

"Danyil, can you promise me something?" Lera began when there were no other people around.

"What is it, Lera?"

"When the time comes, you know, when those savage orcs get here and start killing us all, I don't want to die alone. Mum and dad are gone. I'd like to have at least you nearby in my final moments."

"I will never leave your side, dear sister. Wherever one of us goes, the other will go as well."

"Thanks, Danyil. It's at least a small bit of comfort knowing that I won't be alone when I die."

"I'll do all I can to make sure we do not die," Danyil refused to accept defeat. "I'll find a way for us to escape the city."

A few of the people in the shelter began going topside and exiting the shelter. It seemed it was safe to go out for the time being. Danyil glanced in the direction of the exit and then at the supplies in the room.

"I think it'd be best for us to get some more water and food," he recommended. "We're running low, and who knows for how long we'll be stuck here again when the shelling resumes."

Lera agreed and the two of them began preparing to go topside as well. They grabbed backpacks and a couple of large plastic containers for water and finally got out of the shelter. It was morning time, although life all around was gradually dying more and more. There were more signs of destruction now than the last time they were out. It was overpoweringly depressing.

On each street that they passed, they saw something destroyed. The city was falling apart and being erased from the face of the Earth. Nobody could live anymore in many of these buildings. Danyil began imagining how much effort and money would be needed to restore the whole city. Was it even possible to restore it at all? It seemed that all the damage was irreversible and the city would never be the same as it once was.

Suddenly they heard an ear-piercing shriek of a missile in the air followed by a vociferous fear-inducing explosion somewhere not far away. Danyil and Lera felt the shockwave and the ground shake. They had to stop and brace themselves whilst looking at the skies and checking if any more missiles were coming down.

"That landed very close," Lera said to her brother.

"Let's go and see where it hit. People might be needing help," Danyil said, and without waiting for his sister's response, he ran in the direction of the explosion that just occurred.

Lera ran after her brother. Danyil had an acute feeling that something really terrible had happened just now. He was getting really anxious, expecting to see the devastation any moment now. And then, moments later he saw it. The big drama theatre in the city was aflame, pillars of smoke coming from it, and people running out of it filled with terror.

Danyil and Lera stopped for a moment when they saw the scene. The fires were ferocious and parts of the building were collapsing in front of their eyes.

"There are people trapped inside," Danyil said.

"Danyil, don't go in. It's dangerous!" Lera already knew what her brother was thinking.

"I must!"

Danyil put the container he was carrying down, took his backpack off, and ran towards one of the entrances of the burning building. The fire hadn't yet reached the lower floors and survivors were still running out of the entrance, covered in dust and soot. They were all ordinary innocent civilians with kids. They were terrified and in shock. Some were in tears, trying to find their loved ones but to no avail.

Danyil reached one of the entrances and felt clouds of smoke coming towards him, making him cough uncontrollably. He saw a few bits of rubble falling all over the place. Screams were coming from inside. But which direction were they coming from?

Danyil chaotically turned in various directions and then saw a group of people unable to get past some of the debris, attempting to push it out of the way. Danyil hastily ran to them to help. The fallen debris was heavy and some of it was even burning. No matter how much Danyil tried to avoid the fires, he found himself getting his hands singed a couple of times. When the debris budged a little bit, the survivors on the other side could squeeze through and began coming out one by one. One of them stopped by Danyil's side.

"Don't go in there, fella. It's too dangerous. Come on, we need to get out of here!"

Danyil wanted to see if more people needed help, but the hot smoke that filled the area was choking him and burning his eyes, so he had to give in and agree with the man's suggestion. They ran straight for the exit along with the others before more debris collapsed all around, almost landing on their heads.

16th of March
Somewhere near Kherson

The door swung sharply open, snapping Taras from his inner monologue whilst he and the other prisoners were held in the small, cramped room. Two Russian soldiers stood at the door, gazing around at all the prisoners.

"You!" one of them pointed at Taras.

"This will be a terrible day for me, but I am ready for what's to come," he thought. Taras immediately understood what this was all about. It was one of the daily beatings. Every day for the past week, the captors would randomly choose two or three prisoners, take them to another room and brutally beat them up there. And now Taras understood his turn had finally come.

Taras and one other prisoner were taken out of the room before the door was slammed shut. Two of them were led through the hallway and then down a dark corridor by a group of soldiers. Three of the soldiers then separated the other prisoner and took him to one of the rooms, whilst the other three soldiers led Taras into another room.

The room they led him into was small, dark and stank of dampness. Its walls were cracked and chipped everywhere and there was no furniture or other objects in it.

Before he could turn around to face his captors, he felt a sudden strike to the back of the head with what seemed like the back end of a rifle. Despite the force of the strike, he didn't lose his balance and remained standing. However, a second after that, a punch came directly to his stomach, forcing him to fall to his knees. As he swung his eyes back open, trying his best to withstand the sharp pain, he saw the butt of a rifle just as it struck him square in the face.

Before Taras could fully realise what had happened, he found himself already laying on his back on the filthy floor. His head was spinning and his vision was blurry. Three Russian soldiers were all standing around him and gazing down.

"Told you this guy isn't so hard to take down," one of the soldiers told another. "He's just as pathetic as the rest of them."

The next moment the soldier began kicking and stomping Taras in the ribs and the other two followed straight after. Taras had to bring his arms closer to his chest to try and stop most of the blows from landing in his chest or stomach. His arms were pretty big and he managed to cover himself fully and get into a ball shape, so the soldiers then began kicking him in the back.

When the kicking stopped, Taras breathed out deeply, hoping they were done. One of the soldiers grabbed him by the collar and pulled him up to sit up on his knees. The enemy soldier then brought his own face close to Taras', looking him in the eyes with disdain.

"You like fighting for the Nazi government, don't you?" the Russian soldier asked in a scornful voice.

Taras did not reply. It was no point. No matter what he said, they'd beat him anyway, so he saved his energy. As he turned his eyes towards another soldier, he saw that soldier taking a sharp step towards him, and the next moment he felt a hard boot against his face. The kick knocked Taras backward onto his back. He could taste his own blood at this point. But he refused to give up. They could beat him as much as they wanted, but they would never break his spirit. He was a survivor and he would endure any punishment and humiliation, and when the time was right, he would make them regret ever stepping foot on Ukrainian soil.

16th of March
Kharkiv

Ksenia and Vadym were driving back home from a shop. Olesya stayed at home as they didn't want her to strain herself. The last few days there was a lot of shelling in Kharkiv and the streets were dangerous. They decided it was best to stay sheltered for the time being and at the same time to let Olesya recover before attempting to leave the city. As food at home was almost finished, Ksenia and Vadym decided to go to the shop and resupply. The choices of food were very limited in most shops and they had to settle for buying cheaper, longer-lasting, but also more bland food.

As their car made the next turn in the road, they saw a few guards up ahead checking every car that was passing by. It appeared to be akin to a small checkpoint. There were several checkpoints all over the city now. Vadym wanted to turn back, but it was too late at this point as two more cars were now following behind them along the same road. Their only choice was to carry on ahead towards the checkpoint.

As they got closer to the checkpoint, they saw a little scuffle happening. A driver from the car ahead was ordered by the checkpoint guards to step out of the vehicle, but after stepping out, he struck the nearest guard in the face and attempted to flee. Two other guards ran after the troublemaker and within seconds tackled him down to the ground, at which point they began to handcuff him.

"What was that all about? It looked really serious," Ksenia wondered.

"He must be a saboteur," Vadym concluded. "Likely working for the enemy. The guards must've been made aware of who to look for and recognized him."

When the situation cleared up and one of the guards led the handcuffed man away, two other guards motioned for them to come closer. Vadym brought the car a few metres forward and brought down the window.

The guards wanted to check their ID, and then without any more questions, let them through. Ksenia was glad that one more saboteur working for the enemy was caught, but this got her thinking that there must have been many more still operating in the city and feeding valuable information to the enemy. The enemy then used that information to bomb places in the city. It was worrying to realise that there were many such collaborators all over the city and the country as a whole.

"You know what Anton's dream always was?" Vadym began once they fully cleared the checkpoint, "He always told me how he wanted to open an animal shelter for homeless animals. He loved animals since he was a kid and had a heart of gold. And now my son is gone. Gone forever."

Vadym was getting tearful when he was saying that. It was a huge tragedy for him to lose one of his children and he was still very much struggling to accept it. He continued:

"First it was their mother that I lost, and now Anton. Olesya is the only one I've got left in my life. If God forbid she dies, I'll have no-one else to live for."

"Why did their mother leave to live in Moscow?" Ksenia was very curious. "Olesya and Anton always avoided the subject and didn't want to talk about her, saying that she abandoned them."

"Shortly after their mother Ulyana and I divorced, she married another man. That man later moved back to Moscow and she went to live with him. She tried to get both Olesya and Anton to go with her, but they wanted to stay in Ukraine. She used to be a big part of their lives before her move, but after she left to live in Moscow, she didn't participate in their lives much anymore. She wasn't there during the big events in their lives, and so they stopped expecting anything from her. They understood that she had another life and another child to look after."

"That's quite a pity," Ksenia commented, feeling even more sympathy for her friends than before. "I always believed that both parents should be present in the lives of the children."

"I believe so too, Ksenia. It's why I tried to do everything I could for my children. I wanted to overcompensate for the fact they had only one parent in their lives on a permanent basis. And right now I failed Anton and almost failed Olesya too."

"You did the best you could for them both. I am sure Olesya is grateful to you for everything, and Anton likely would've been too if he was still with us."

"Maybe. I always feel I could've done more. But I don't know."

He went silent there, lost in his thoughts. Ksenia did not want to press him further about the subject as it was quite obviously a sensitive subject to him.

Once back at home, they brought the bags of groceries in and began unpacking them. Olesya helped them out. Ksenia told her about what they saw on the way back, how a possible conspirator was caught at a mini-checkpoint right in front of them. She was impressed and wished she was there to see the scene too. Ksenia could see that Olesya was feeling disdainful towards anyone siding with the aggressors and was gaining some delight from news of collaborators being caught.

The sound of the air raid alarm suddenly came on outside. It startled them, but hearing distant explosions startled them even more and they realised they needed to run down to the basement to hide once again. Ksenia and Vadym grabbed several of the packets of food that they bought and followed Olesya out of the apartment and down to the basement, to wait for another wave of missiles to pass.

17th of March
Mariupol

Danyil and Lera were in a clinic. A nurse was doing a follow up check on the burns Danyil received on his hands the day before. She took off the old bandages and began inspecting how the healing was going.

"Danyil, I hope you won't do something like this ever again," Lera told her brother. "You know you could've died there."

"If not for me being there, almost a dozen people could've died."

"I understand, but please don't do reckless things such as this again. I need you, you know."

"I do know it perfectly. Sorry. I just thought I could help other people too. You saw what happened to that theatre building."

"And you did an amazing thing to save some of those people. But please try and not hurt yourself. I beg you."

"All right, I'll try."

The nurse applied some more ointment on his burns and then spoke:

"Your hands should heal quite soon. The burns are not deep. Just a bit swollen, but that will subside."

Danyil was pleased to hear that the burns weren't serious and would heal up soon. He needed to be in top shape at a demanding time such as this.

After the nurse put clean new bandages on the burns, Danyil and Lera left the clinic. A lot of people were coming into the clinic. Most were injured during shelling that had been happening on a daily basis. However, a few started coming in with infections due to drinking contaminated water. Clean water was starting to become incredibly hard to get in the city and many people were drinking unclean water out of desperation.

"Those orcs are slowly choking the life out of this city," Lera commented once they were out of the building. "They're starving us and depriving us of water and basic necessities. There'll be no-one left in the city by the time their troops actually get here. This is a cruel and awful ordeal to put someone through. A slow, agonising and undignified death."

"We need to find a safe passage out of the city," Danyil responded. "I'm going to spend the next few days on that task. It is our only choice, I'm afraid."

"You're going to be walking out and about while shelling is going on?"

"I'll be careful, but yes. Sitting in the shelter and doing nothing – that's just waiting for the death to come. I'm going to find a way. I'm going to ask around and see what I can find."

"Then let me help you, please."

"There's no need to, dear sister. I am only going to be spending a few hours during the day and then will be back in the shelter each evening. It will be easier and faster this way."

Lera sighed and did not persist. Danyil always had his ways of getting things done, and by now his sister learned to trust his methods. However, this was going to be one of the hardest tasks he had ever taken upon himself, maybe even the hardest. Whether he was going to succeed or not, he wasn't sure about, but he was prepared to do anything possible to get his sister out of this hell.

"I hope someday soon we'll walk through beautiful parks again," Lera continued. "I hope we'll watch the sunrise and the sunset, swim in a pool, and just simply enjoy the atmosphere of calm around us. This is what I dream of, Danyil, and I don't want to be alone when that time comes. I can't lose my whole family. You understand?"

"I understand, my dear sister. I understand."

18th of March
Mykolaiv

Solomiya was staring in horror at the sight in front of her. One of the barracks buildings in Mykolaiv was hit by Russian missiles during the night. Now it wasn't even recognizable as a building anymore. It was just a handful of remains of destroyed walls and a massive pile of rubble – rocks, wooden planks, collapsed roof sections, and lakes of dirt everywhere. It was believed that around two hundred soldiers were inside when this occurred and so far nobody was found alive. The rescuers were only digging dead bodies out of the rubble.

Every person who was part of the rescue team had a deeply glum expression on the face. They kept digging through the rubble, moving big stones and objects aside, only to find more corpses. And yet despite the harshness of the destruction, they continued. If at least one life survived this attack, he or she needed to be saved.

Solomiya arrived at this scene on her way to the hospital. After hearing the news about the attack in the morning, she decided to head there first in case there were wounded people that needed medical help. But from what she could see, so far nobody was found alive. She remained at the scene until the time for her hospital shift came. Once there were already several ambulances and other medics at the scene, she decided it was best to go to her shift.

On her way to the hospital, her parents called her. They had been checking up on her regularly, especially after they heard of what happened to Tymur. Solomiya knew they were worried for her. She didn't want to give them any more stress than they already had, so she always tried her best not to overshare her negative emotions with them. When she reached the hospital, she wished them to stay safe and to have a good day before ending the conversation.

Her main responsibility at the hospital had been to watch over Zlata during the last few days and to make sure the 10-year old girl's condition was stable. Zlata was still unconscious all these days. Solomiya was worrying about her every single day while she was looking after her. Each time she came to her shift, she hoped Zlata would be awake already, but each time it was the same scene. The poor little girl was injured quite severely. *What will she even feel when she wakes up and notices that one of her arms is no longer there?*

"How's she today?" Vira, the senior nurse, walked into the ward and snapped Solomiya from her thoughts.

"Still in the same state. Although at least she's stable and recovering," Solomiya replied.

"Good. I believe she's past the worst already."

"You think she'll get back to her senses in a couple of days?"

"It's hard to say how soon that will happen, but let's hope for the best. Keep up the good work, Solomiya. If anything changes about her condition, let me or another colleague know."

Vira left and Solomiya turned back to monitor the girl's condition. She had to make regular notes of any changes or lack thereof and to make sure that the life support continued to operate properly.

She kept on experiencing very strong feelings towards this little girl, wishing with every part of herself that Zlata would wake up soon and recover fully. She couldn't stand seeing children suffer so severely, and she knew that Zlata was by far not the only child to have suffered in this war.

After a few minutes she exited the room into the corridor as she needed to get a few supplies. When in the corridor, she noticed something that escaped her when she first came in that day. Lots of body bags with corpses inside were stacked in the corridors. It looked like there was no storage space for the dead and the situation had only been getting worse over the last couple of weeks. *Were there really so many people dying in the city?* She knew that a lot of wounded soldiers were being brought into the hospital since the start of the invasion, including soldiers of the enemy. Pavel was the only Russian soldier she treated so far, but she knew that other nurses had to treat many others.

She began wondering if the situation at the front was getting worse and if Mykolaiv would fall soon. It would be in complete contrast to the social media posts by Vitaliy Kim, the governor of Mykolaiv oblast, who had been always posting encouraging announcements and making this hell seem a lot less scary than initially expected. But was all that just a way to soften the blow that would come in the near future or maybe things indeed weren't as bad as they could had been. Maybe the fact that Mykolaiv was still fighting back was a sign that the enemy was not unstoppable. Time would only show what would happen next.

Solomiya started to feel a cold sweat on her forehead from all the worrying and decided that she'd keep these thoughts as far away from herself as possible. She was not a soldier and could not do anything about the military side of things. All she could do was to make sure that people in her care would survive and recover from their injuries.

20th of March
Outskirts of Kyiv

Two vehicles arrived in a small settlement just on the outskirts of Kyiv. Oleksiy and Dmytro were part of a team tasked to deliver supplies to the frontline, as well as to the ordinary people living in the settlement.

"They said this area was liberated only a few days ago," Oleksiy mentioned to Dmytro as they both got out of the supply vehicle. "The enemy forces have been pushed back but not far. It's going to be very dangerous here."

"We'll be fine, brother. Let's just watch each other's backs."

Oleksiy found it surprising that his friend was not nervous at all to be all the way out here, so close to the frontline. He couldn't understand if Dmytro was fully grasping the level of danger in this region or not.

Two men got out of the other vehicle as well. Oleksiy and Dmytro walked up to them to get instructions. One of the men was in charge and began explaining:

"So here's the plan. We'll need to split up. The two of you will distribute supplies in the western parts of this settlement and the two of us will do so in the eastern parts. The bags are labelled, so make sure you take the right ones. The remaining ones we'll have to take even closer to the frontline, which is a little further north. All understood?"

Oleksiy and Dmytro agreed to do as they were told and began unloading the bags from the vehicles. The supplies mainly consisted of basic food and medicines, the things that ordinary people desperately needed and were short on. Once they grabbed the bags, they headed to the part of the settlement where they were told to distribute the supplies. They had to knock on the doors and directly hand the essential supplies to the people living in each home.

Oleksiy was gaining a sense of satisfaction from doing this. He felt that he was doing something helpful and making a difference at an incredibly hard and depressing time for the country. Ordinary people were living through a nightmare, and every little bit of help could make a difference in their lives - every medicine delivered to a sick person or a sandwich given to a child who ate hardly anything all day. Some people's homes were damaged, but they continued staying in them, refusing to abandon what little shelter they had left and trying to get by as best as they could.

"You know, if so many people here need help, imagine how many more are out there in the territories that are still occupied and who are waiting patiently for help to arrive," Oleksiy spoke out loud a thought that hit him.

"The whole of Ukraine is crying, brother. Even people in territories that were never occupied are suffering," Dmytro responded.

"Yes, you are right. But when you see that people in some places aren't even getting the basic essentials, it makes you think. It's very humbling I must say."

"Don't think too much. Just do what you feel is best. That's what my motto has always been."

Oleksiy nodded in agreement and in the next moment they reached a fork in the road. There were houses lined up along each road that was coming off from the fork.

"What do you think? You take one of the streets and I take another?" Oleksiy suggested.

"Sounds good. Let's do that and meet at the next junction."

They split up. Oleksiy continued as before, knocking on the door of each house along both sides of the road and offering useful essentials to the people living there. There were a lot of homes to get through, but he was not in a rush. He wanted to make sure every person was helped.

Suddenly an ear-splitting, screeching whistle of a missile was heard and followed by a bang. Then a screech again. And another bang. The ground was shaking. The air around Oleksiy was panicking. Another screech came, followed by another bang. He turned around to its sound and saw a top part of one of the buildings in the distance beginning to crumble apart into pieces. The area was getting shelled and it must have been happening from a somewhat short distance away as the air raid alarm hadn't even kicked in yet.

Oleksiy quickly got a hold of his senses and took control of his panic. He had to get into cover immediately or else he'd become a casualty. Two more screeches pierced his ears and he saw two missiles flying overhead, scratching the sky and slamming into something in the distance. He didn't realise that his feet were already running, although he had no idea where. Frantically, he began looking in every direction around him, hoping to find a shelter. He didn't want to risk barging into anyone's home uninvited, but the thought began to nag him as more missiles whistled through the air above and landed somewhere not too far.

A narrow alleyway! His eyes focused on a little gap between two houses. He ran into the alleyway, still carrying the bag full of supplies. It was a little bit safer inside an alleyway, but he wanted to find a way underground or at least inside a building.

He spotted a worn down wooden door on the side of one of the buildings. He attempted to pull it and to his surprise it swung open without any resistance. And directly ahead – steps leading down into a cellar. Perfect! Oleksiy heard more resonant banging from missile impacts and hurried inside and down the wooden steps. The steps, however, began creaking and singing dissonant notes under his feet until a whole section of the staircase snapped and broke from under his feet. Oleksiy felt himself getting pulled down through the broken steps. As he fell, he was met by a hard ground underneath which knocked him completely out.

Chapter 7

21st of March
Bucha

Maria and Alina felt themselves a lot safer whilst staying at Georgiy's house. It was rare for Russian soldiers to show up there. Most times they were only passing along the road some distance away from the house. And yet Maria felt exceedingly worried as their situation was uncertain, and after seeing the horrors the enemy did to her husband and neighbours, she couldn't get her nerves under control and kept having persistent nightmares.

Early morning came and Maria was ready to go and prepare breakfast for everyone. It was still 5:30 in the morning, but she and her daughter were up already. Georgiy was also up, fixing a few things in his house. Maria glanced out of the window as she often did, constantly looking out for danger. As though her fears came back to haunt her, she spotted two Russian soldiers approaching the house from afar. They were coming here and this was unmistakeable. Her heartbeat accelerated and her hands went cold. Then she looked a bit closer and recognized one of the soldiers. It was the same one who murdered her husband.

"Georgiy, soldiers are coming," she alerted him.

"That's strange of them to come," Georgiy wondered. "They usually expect me to be there to do the digging at 7 am. It's still too early."

"Maybe they found something out. Maybe this is regarding those two men that tried to rape me. My daughter and I need to hide! I recognize one of the soldiers!"

"All right, just go over to that storage room over there," Georgiy pointed with his finger, "and close the door. You should be safe there. I'll try to find out what they want."

Maria felt panic taking over and she began to fear for her own and her daughter's lives once again. That horrible feeling came back, even though it was subsiding over the last few days. She realised that perhaps a sense of terror would never truly leave her alone until her dying breath.

Both Maria and Alina rushed into the storage room, closing the door behind themselves. Maria sat down, her breathing was fast and heavy. Alina came closer to her and hugged her. She could see how worried her mother was. Maria hugged her back and didn't want to let go off her daughter, afraid that something might happen to them both.

A knock on the front door then came. Maria stopped breathing so hard and listened in. She could hear Georgiy opening the door and greeting the soldiers. She got up and walked closer to the door so that she could better hear what was being said.

"We've been tasked to collect some food and need to see what you have," one of the soldiers said.

"You are free to look, but I don't have much," Georgiy answered to their request.

"You must have plenty of canned food. Where do you keep it?"

"In the kitchen."

Maria then heard footsteps. The kitchen was directly next to the storage room where she and Alina were hiding. She could hear the soldiers even more clearly now but couldn't see what was going on. Most of the sounds were those of small objects being moved around with impatience.

"Is that all of it?" one of the soldiers asked after sifting through a cabinet.

"Yes."

"Fine. That will do."

Maria took a small step back from the door causing a floorboard beneath her to audibly creak. She froze in place, hoping nobody heard that.

"Who's in that room?" one of the soldiers questioned.

"It's uh…" Georgiy began, but he was stopped by the soldiers as their footsteps were now approaching closer.

Maria felt terrified but quickly composed herself. She knelt down and began pretending that she's looking for something in the nearby boxes.

The storage room door was sharply opened by one of the soldiers, who then peered inside. Maria got up on her feet and turned towards him, seeing the face of a man who was responsible for killing her husband. She tried her best to withhold her emotions so not to cause any changes in her facial expression.

"Sorry," Georgiy quickly began thinking of an excuse, "my daughter has been helping me around the house."

"Hmm, have I not seen you somewhere before?" the soldier said suspiciously.

The other soldier also came closer; he was shorter in height. They both stood in the doorway, looking inside.

"I… I don't think so," Maria murmured quietly whilst looking down at the floor.

"I swear I saw you living a few streets down from here. I remember your daughter too. In fact, that idiot Pasternak kept talking about you non-stop, saying what he wanted to do to you. And he's dead now, which raises questions. I'd like you to come with us."

A scorching feeling of fear appeared in her stomach and began to pierce her every organ. She didn't know what to do. She didn't want to be taken away by them. They would likely torture her, rape her and then kill her.

At that moment Maria saw Georgiy taking a swing with a crowbar and striking the shorter of the two soldiers to the back of the head with great force. The strike brought the soldier down in less than a second, but this alerted the taller soldier who was questioning Maria.

"You fucking bastard!" the tall soldier yelled as he turned around and saw what happened.

Georgiy swung the crowbar again, this time towards the second soldier. The soldier attempted to dodge the strike, although it landed on his shoulder with the curved end of the crowbar. He grunted from pain but brought his rifle up regardless to aim at Georgiy. Georgiy tried to push the soldier over, but the soldier overpowered him and began pushing him the other way, towards the kitchen. The two of them fell down, locked together, with the soldier on top. The end of the crowbar was still jammed in the shoulder of the Russian soldier, but the strength had not left him. Georgiy was trying to push the crowbar deeper into him, but his enemy was too strong. He aimed his rifle right at Georgiy's stomach and shot several rounds at point blank range.

Each shot that was fired made Maria and Alina jump in terror. Maria realised that she only had a couple of seconds to react before the soldier would attempt to attack her. She rushed into the kitchen out of pure survival instinct, grabbed a big knife that was on the kitchen table and thrust it towards the soldier from behind. The knife entered deep into his back between the shoulder blades, causing the Russian soldier to drop his weapon and stop moving with the only exception of an uncontrollable shake of his hands. A few seconds later the enemy soldier collapsed onto the ground beside Georgiy.

Maria needed a few moments to catch her breath. Her heart was beating so forcefully that it felt like it was about to burst out of her chest. She could feel herself sweating and her limbs were vibrating on accord of their own.

"Mum?" Alina's voice came from the storage room.

"It's ok, darling. Just stay there," Maria responded whilst still trying to catch her breath. She did not want her daughter to see this. Georgiy was already dead. There was no more life in his eyes. He took a risk to save their lives and paid for it with his own.

Maria's legs felt weak and she had to sit down on the floor. She couldn't gain control of her panic. Even though both Russian soldiers were dead, her whole body was still firing off a constant sense of alarm. She lay down on the floor in a foetal position and began to sob. She needed to let these emotions out and it had to happen right now.

Alina entered the kitchen and saw her mother crying on the floor. She ran to her mother's side and gently caressed her shoulder.

"Mum, what's wrong? Did they hurt you? Mum, please."

"No, no. They didn't hurt me, my darling. Just give me a moment."

Alina began crying too whilst seeing her mother like this. She lay down next to Maria and hugged her. The two of them continued laying together in a tight embrace for a couple of minutes.

"We're going to have to leave this place, dear," Maria told her daughter when she finally managed to stop herself from crying. "It's unsafe for us. They will send more soldiers to see why these ones have not come back."

"Ok mum, I understand."

"Let's gather everything that's useful and go. Make sure to put something warm on. It's still cold out there."

Alina nodded in understanding as both of them got up from the floor. Without delay they began filling a bag with food and other useful supplies for the road. Maria did not know where they would run, but they had to get out of this place, they had to get out of the occupied territory at all costs.

21st of March
Outskirts of Kyiv

Oleksiy regained his consciousness. There was dust everywhere – his mouth, his nose, his eyes. As he acquired strength in his limbs, he used his hands to brush the dust off his face so that he could open his eyes fully. His vision was blurred and his head was aching a fair bit. A thin ray of sunlight was coming through the open doorway up above through which he entered the cellar, but other than that it was very dim inside.

After applying some effort, Oleksiy lifted his heavy head and looked around, still trying to remember where he was. A few moments later he remembered what happened and attempted to sit up. His head spun even more now and he needed a handful of seconds to readjust his sense of balance.

"How long have I been out? Is it morning already?" he asked himself.

When he felt confident enough, he got onto his feet very carefully and looked all around the dimly-lit cellar. Because a large part of the wooden stairs broke, he figured he wouldn't be able to go back out that way. There was another set of stairs here; that one was leading further into the building. Oleksiy wasted no time and headed up along the steps. To his relief these were stone steps and he was sure they wouldn't collapse from under him.

At the end of the stairs there was a door. He pushed it open without much trouble and was now inside a two-storey house. It appeared that the building was hit by one of the missiles from the day before. Parts of the ceiling were broken completely, and Oleksiy could see the sky through the large holes in it. Down below on the floor level there was rubble scattered everywhere. The windows were all shattered and tiny pieces of glass were polluting the whole floor.

The house appeared to have been abandoned. Its owners must have left it earlier on during the invasion or perhaps even before it. A few objects of furniture were still there, but it was obvious that no-one was at home for days.

Or was that so? Oleksiy heard a gentle whimpering noise. It sounded like a dog. He looked towards the direction of the sound, but couldn't see anything. There was just rubble. He knelt down and gazed under it and saw a dog trapped under a handful of wooden beams and planks. He hastily grabbed the first couple of wooden beams and threw them aside, then another one, and another. Once he removed the bulk of the fallen debris, the dog squeezed itself out of the narrow gap. It was a German Shepherd breed and didn't seem to be fully grown yet. Perhaps about a year or two of age.

"Hey," Oleksiy stroked the dog gently as it came closer to him to show appreciation, "were you just left here by yourself? Where are your owners?"

The dog just sat down and gazed at him, its tongue hanging out. Oleksiy got up from the floor and turned in the direction of the front door. There was no point losing time. He needed to find Dmytro and the others. They were likely looking for him.

As he approached the front door, the dog followed him. The door was locked. However, it could be opened from the inside without a key. Oleksiy unlocked it and opened it. The dog followed him out.

"You want to come with me or something? What about your owners?" he asked.

The dog continued looking at him, a friendly and affectionate expression on its face.

"Ok fine. You can come with me if you'd like. What should I call you? Is it ok if I call you Max? I always thought if I had a dog, that's the name I'd give it."

He decided to get going. As he looked around, he noticed a few buildings were damaged that were fine the day before. The damage evidently happened due to yesterday's attack. Fresh bits of rubble were now lying beside the buildings.

He wasn't sure where Dmytro could had been at that moment in time, but decided that it was best to head to the place where they parked their vehicles. At some point either Dmytro or the other two guys would return to the cars, so it seemed like a logical meeting point.

As he walked further along the road, he saw Dmytro in the distance. It seemed he found his friend even sooner than he had expected. He hastened his step. Max was following close behind him. Dmytro turned in his direction and saw him as he got closer, a sense of relief appearing on his face.

"Oleksiy, brother, where the hell have you been? And what happened to you?"

"I tried to find a shelter yesterday when the shelling started," Oleksiy began explaining, "but then I fell down through some stairs and lost my senses."

"We've been looking for you all evening yesterday after the shelling stopped. Glad you're all right. I was worried you got buried under a rubble somewhere."

"Sorry to keep you worried."

"And what's this? You've made a new friend?" Dmytro pointed at the dog.

"That's Max. He was trapped under some rubble in the same house where I took shelter. Not sure where his owners are, but he seems to be following me around."

"Ha, funny. Dogs always did love you. But anyway, let's return to the cars. We still need to deliver some of the supplies closer to the frontline."

Dmytro turned around and began walking back, with Oleksiy and Max following him. The moment Dmytro began walking, something caught Oleksiy's eye on the ground.

"Dmytro, wait, sto-"

Oleksiy did not get a chance to finish warning his friend of what he saw when a small but very loud explosion occurred right where Dmytro stepped, violently knocking him to the side and onto the ground. It was one of the small unexploded bomblets that came from a cluster bomb. Dmytro accidentally stepped on it without noticing, and this prompted it to detonate. Now Dmytro was laying on the ground, clutching onto his leg and hoarsely screaming from pain. Smoke was everywhere at the site of the explosion. Oleksiy rushed to his friend's side despite nearly getting knocked down by the shockwave of the explosion.

Dmytro couldn't open his eyes. He was just writhing from an unbearable pain. His whole left leg was charred and burning, and Oleksiy could even see the boot was torn apart by the explosion.

"Dmytro, stay with me!" he shouted to get his friend's attention.

Dmytro desperately needed paramedics, but there was nobody around. Only a few civilians ran closer to observe what had happened.

"We need some medics here! Quickly!" Oleksiy yelled towards the group of people that began gathering.

Some of the people immediately scurried to find some help. A couple of others hurriedly came closer to help keep Dmytro stable.

"Don't you dare to give up, brother! The help will be here any moment now!" Oleksiy kept saying.

He knew Dmytro could hear him despite screaming from an enormous pain and still being unable to open his eyes. Oleksiy continued frantically looking around, hoping the help would get here soon. Every second was precious, and Dmytro's condition was critical. He could pass out at any moment if not helped in time.

22nd of March
Somewhere near Kherson

Taras and Roman were sitting at a small wooden table and having their meal. It was dinner time and the other prisoners were also in the canteen, having some food to keep themselves going through their ordeal. Taras was immersed in thoughts. He really missed his family. He wanted to see them again or at least to hear their voices. He had not spoken to them since the day Kherson was taken and he was captured as a prisoner. They had no idea if he was still alive or not, and this was gnawing at him, making him feel restless. He did not want them to suffer emotionally. He wished he could at least send a message their way, just to tell them that he was still alive, to give them a peace of mind.

His thoughts were interrupted by an unpleasant sound of something falling onto the floor. He and Roman looked in the direction of the sound and saw one of the Russian soldiers deliberately having dropped some food on the floor.

"You there, pick it up!" the Russian soldier commanded one of the prisoners and pushed him onto the floor.

"These bastards are making me sick," Roman commented quietly so only Taras could hear him.

"Patience, friend. They'll regret everything. I promise you that."

Both of them finished their meal, grabbed their rubbish and got up. They threw the rubbish in the nearby bin and then, without disturbing anyone and without making eye contact with any Russian soldier, they left the canteen and into the main hallway.

Taras sat down on one of the seats where he could oversee the whole hallway. He liked inspecting it for details. Roman was not far, walking around and looking for anything useful. They had to stay inconspicuous and not draw attention to themselves. Taras had been preparing to turn this place upside down and to free all the captives, but to do that, he needed to be aware of every important detail in the building and to really get to know the enemy soldiers and their habits. Unfortunately some of the soldiers were swapped for new ones every now and again, and so he had to learn about the new ones from scratch.

Despite that, the number of soldiers overseeing the prisoners was always the same. He counted that there had been exactly 12 Russian soldiers in the barracks at all times. Each one was armed with an assault rifle, but Taras suspected that most weren't well-trained. The best soldiers wouldn't be tasked with a guard duty and instead would be sent fighting.

He noticed that in the afternoon time, all 12 soldiers were out and about, but in the morning time, only 9 were. This suggested that the other three were most likely sleeping at that time, which could mean that they were the night-shift soldiers, watching over the barracks when everyone else slept.

So, for a successful breakout, night time was more ideal, when more soldiers were asleep. The trouble was that at night all the prisoners were kept in their small room the entire time and the door was locked. So if they wanted to break out at night, they needed a way to lure one of the night-shift soldiers to open the door.

"You two, over here," Taras heard one of the Russian soldiers commanding.

He diverted his gaze to check if the soldier was talking to him and noticed that the soldier was facing the other way and talking to the only two female prisoners who had just exited the canteen. The soldier demanded for them to go and stand in another part of the main hallway where three other Russian soldiers were standing.

"Now, both of you, take your clothes off," the soldier demanded.

"What?"

"You heard me right. Strip down to your underwear."

The two women had a despondent look on their faces, realising they were about to be humiliated and treated as nothing more than pieces of meat. Reluctantly they did as they were told and took their clothes off, only keeping the underwear on.

"Who said this job sucked? It's great really, so long as we get beauties like these here," one of the Russian soldiers commented.

"They're a bit skinny. We should feed them more," another one responded.

"Darlings, why don't you turn around... slowly," the first soldier instructed the two women.

Taras could not watch this. He could feel everything the two women prisoners were feeling, wishing he could beat those perverted enemy soldiers to a pulp right here right now. Unfortunately there was little he could do right now. The soldiers were well-armed and he'd only get himself beaten up or killed if he did anything reckless.

"Can I touch them?" Taras heard one of the soldiers asking another one.

"Don't get too carried away, ok?" the other replied sternly.

Taras refused to look at what was happening, but he could hear everything. He could hear every demeaning word spoken by the Russian soldiers. Those women had nerves of steel to endure all of that without startIng to cry or beg to be left alone. They simply put up with all the humiliation.

Then something else caught his attention. One of the other Russian soldiers was standing just some distance behind Taras and listening to the radio transmissions from another military unit. They were talking about their offensive towards Mykolaiv and how it wasn't going well. Taras heard everything and felt relieved. Roman joined back with him half a minute later, sitting right next to him.

"You heard that?" Taras asked Roman in an almost whispering voice.

"Heard what?"

"What they were talking about on their radio. Mykolaiv is still fighting back. They've not managed to take it."

"That's good news, right?"

"Of course. We now know where we could go for help once we get out of here. If Mykolaiv is not in their control, it means we're not that far behind enemy lines."

"That's true. But first we must find a way of getting out of here."

"It will happen in time," Taras said confidently. "Did you find anything else that could be useful?"

"Yeah," Roman said. He gazed around to check on every Russian soldier in the hallway. When he noticed that none of them were looking in his direction, he brought one of his feet up onto the seat and slightly lifted one of his trouser leggings for a brief second before hiding it again. Taras managed to see a big, sharp glass shard sticking slightly out of Roman's boot.

"Ok, that's perfect. We'll need more objects like this. Let's try to find anything we can in the next few days."

"I'll be on it like a hawk."

Taras mustered the strength to look again at the scene involving the two women prisoners. It appeared that the soldiers were bored of ogling at the women, and both women were in the process of putting their clothes back on. One of the enemy soldiers then walked over to the doorway leading to the canteen and yelled at everyone remaining in it to hurry up eating because the dinner time was over and it was time to get back in the tiny room for the night.

Solomiya came into the hospital early in the morning to start her shift. The days continued being identical to one another, and nothing appeared to be changing. Things only continued to get more difficult with each day as more wounded people were brought to the hospital. Solomiya began to accept a scary possibility that the war might not end any time soon and the difficult time for her and her country could continue for many more months. She thought if only Tymur was still alive, then at least going through this hell together with him would've been a little bit easier. But facing it all alone was unquestionably terrifying.

As per her usual schedule of the last two weeks, she went straight to the ward where Zlata was to take over from another nurse. As Solomiya entered the room, she saw two nurses sitting by the little girl's bed and the girl was awake. *Has she finally regained her senses?* Solomiya could not believe her eyes. For two weeks she kept coming to the hospital and looking after Zlata; nothing was changing and Zlata continued being unconscious. And now, finally, she was awake.

"She's awake?" Solomiya repeated her thoughts.

The two nurses turned in her direction.

"She's literally woken up just a minute ago. It's like she felt your arrival or something," one of the nurses replied.

The girl still looked rather poorly. She kept looking around in confusion, a very sad expression on her face.

"What's happening to her?"

"She's just having a little shock and trying to understand where she is."

Solomiya came closer to the girl's bed and sat next to it as well, along with the other two nurses.

"Hey, how are you feeling?" she asked.

Zlata did not respond, but she stopped looking around the place and focused her eyes on Solomiya. Solomiya leaned in closer and put her hand on Zlata's shoulder.

"Hey, it's ok. You're safe here," she consoled the 10-year old.

"How did I get here?" Zlata asked all of a sudden.

"Your home was hit, but you're safe now. Don't worry, ok?"

Zlata's eyes then looked down and she saw herself in a hospital bed and then she saw in horror that her left arm was gone.

"Where is my arm? Where?"

Fear overtook her and she began to cry uncontrollably, asking what happened to her arm repeatedly. Solomiya came closer and put her arms around the poor girl, giving her a warm and gentle hug. She didn't say anything as nothing she could say would make Zlata feel any better. One of the girl's arms was gone for good and there was no denying that horrible fact. All she could do was show utmost care and love for the child to help her get through this trauma on an emotional level. The worse news was yet to come. The girl did not know yet that her parents were dead, and Solomiya was still clueless as to how she would break those news to her.

"We should get you something to eat. Are you hungry?" one of the other nurses asked Zlata.

Zlata shook her head. Solomiya could understand that the girl would have no appetite whilst seeing what happened to her. She needed time to calm down and for the emotions to subside a bit.

"You should eat something," Solomiya told her a few moments later. "You need the strength, dear."

"I don't want to eat. I want to go home and see my mum and dad."

"You need to stay here, dear, so that you can recover. We're all here for you, ok?"

Zlata lowered her eyes, tears continued falling down her cheeks.

"Can I at least see mum and dad? Are they here?"

Solomiya briefly closed her eyes as she feared this moment would come. She did not know what to say and was at an absolute loss for words.

"They're not here, dear," one of the other nurses said after a brief pause.

"When will they come? Can I talk to them on the phone? Did they also get hurt?"

There were so many questions. The little girl was understandably very concerned and wanted to be with her parents at this highly vulnerable for her time. The two other nurses in the room looked at each other and then at Solomiya. None of them knew what to say and how to answer.

"They got hurt, didn't they?" Zlata could tell by their reaction.

"Sorry, dear," one of the nurses said without adding any more details.

The girl still had no idea her parents were gone. How should they tell this to her? She was still feeling physically weak. The news of her parents no longer being with her would destroy her and impact her recovery.

Seeing that the nurses weren't telling her anything else, Zlata lay her upper body back down on the pillow and turned to the side as much as she could. She gazed at the bandaged up stomp that was in place of her left arm, still trying hard to accept that as her new reality.

Solomiya and the other two nurses stepped away from the girl's bed into another corner of the room, discussing how to tell the girl about her parents.

"We should wait a few days," Solomiya suggested, making sure to keep her voice down. "We need to let her recover a bit more first."

"Sooner or later she'll ask to see them again," another nurse mentioned. "We can't keep this a secret from her forever."

"I know. We should give her at least a couple more days. One step at a time. Let her adjust to the shock. She's just realised she's in a hospital and is missing an arm."

They agreed this was the best course of action for now. In a meantime they needed to make sure that she continued making a physical recovery.

Solomiya was glad that Zlata had finally woken up from her coma. This was a huge step forward in the girl's recovery. She thought for a moment how it was the same with her own heart, how losing Tymur sent her emotions into a state of coma, and that now she was gradually recovering. She knew that just as the little girl's injuries, the scars in her own heart would always be there and she would always miss her beloved, but perhaps she could at least move forward through life and not be crippled by the pain in her heart.

23rd of March
Outskirts of Kyiv

Maria and Alina kept going for over two days now. Maria had no idea where they were. She didn't have a map, and her phone was taken from her by the Russian soldiers when they first invaded her home. She didn't know this area at all. The only thought that gave her peace was that she and her daughter were reasonably far away from Bucha now, and the murderers that attacked their suburb would not find them anymore.

It wasn't easy getting out of the occupied territory, as the Russian patrols could appear anywhere, and Maria still didn't know if she was out of the occupied territory or if she ventured even deeper into it. For that reason their progress was slow as they had to pick their timing correctly. Keeping to the forested area seemed safer as they were unlikely to be discovered there, whilst going along the roads was too dangerous.

What made things even worse for Maria was that she twisted her ankle half a day ago and it was aching. Despite the pain and discomfort, she couldn't stop and carried on regardless.

"Mum, where are we going?" Alina asked again. Maria lost count how many times her daughter asked that now.

"To safety, dear. We need to find someone who will help us."

"We've been going for ages."

"Do you need a rest?"

"Yes, please."

They sat down on the grass by some trees. The area was somewhat secluded and surrounded by several trees and bushes. It was peaceful. The sun was setting on the horizon and only a few beams of light were still coming through the gaps between the trees. Maria took a deep breath, feeling the smells of nature and appreciating the fact that she and her daughter were still alive after what they had been through.

"Do you want to eat anything?" Maria asked her daughter.

"Just a little bit," Alina replied.

Maria searched in the backpack and got out one of the sandwiches that she made before they departed from Bucha. This was the last of the sandwiches and now they only had some canned food left and a few waffle bars. She handed the sandwich to her daughter and hoped that they would find some help the next day.

She was feeling very tired and shivery all of a sudden, so she zipped up her coat to try and stay warmer. Her eyes got heavy as she gazed at the evening sky. She leaned her head back against a tree to try and relax. *Maybe we should just spend the night here and continue tomorrow. I can't go on right now...*

Chapter 8

24th of March
Outskirts of Kyiv

Oleksiy continued making deliveries of important supplies along with several other people over the last few days. Now his friend Dmytro was no longer keeping him company. After stepping on an explosive, Dmytro was taken to a hospital to be treated for severe injuries and burns. His life was saved, but unfortunately his left leg could not be saved. It was emotionally difficult. Oleksiy suspected that Dmytro would have to stay in the hospital for the next few days at least. He knew he'd need to check up on his best friend in a few days and to give him some moral support.

For now, he had to do his part in helping the people in recently liberated territories, as well as to the soldiers who were fighting very close to the frontline. At times he was even asked to repair a few things as his skill at repairing vehicles came very useful.

It was a morning time and Oleksiy was in a settlement that was liberated only a day ago. Some Ukrainian soldiers were still patrolling the streets. He along with a few other people were among the first to bring in supplies and humanitarian aid. His new canine friend, Max, was sticking close to him at all times. Shortly after Dmytro was taken to a hospital, Oleksiy found out that the dog's owners had been killed only a few days ago and the dog was left on its own.

Oleksiy spent the next hour delivering the supplies to civilians. As he delivered yet another package of food to people in one of the houses along a quiet road, he began proceeding to the next house when he noticed Max stopped following him and turned away somewhere.

"What is it, Max?" he asked.

The dog continued looking somewhere out beyond the houses and into a wooded area. Then, after a few more seconds, he barked to get Oleksiy's attention and ran in the direction of the woods.

"Max, wait! Where are you going?"

Oleksiy couldn't understand why Max suddenly ran towards the woods, but he decided to follow. Perhaps something of importance was there. Max continued producing a barking noise after every few steps to make sure Oleksiy was following him. Oleksiy ran at the fastest pace he possibly could whilst carrying a bag full of supplies.

Once they were inside the wooded area, it was more difficult for Oleksiy to see Max up ahead. The trees weren't so dense at first, but as they ventured deeper, the trees and other plants got closer together and it was to some degree darker there too. Oleksiy had to dodge lots of prickly shrubs by either side of the path and could hear dry twigs crunching beneath his feet as he continued running after his dog. A few small, hanging branches slapped his face on the way too as the path was rather narrow in places.

Max finally stopped whilst looking someplace to the right. Oleksiy reached him, trying to catch his breath and feeling like all the blood in his body had begun to swirl around in a frenzy. He then heard something and turned in the direction Max was facing. A little girl was in the distance, running this way towards them and yelling for help. Oleksiy waited not a second more and ran to see what was going on. Max ran right after him, barking along the way. The girl saw them and stopped, looking relieved.

"Hey, are you all right?" Oleksiy asked as soon as he reached her.

"I need some help. My mum is not getting up," the girl said whilst shedding tears.

"Where is she?"

"This way."

The girl began running back to where she came from, with Oleksiy and Max following her. They didn't need to travel far, as very soon they came across a patch of trees and shrubs arranged in a sort of semi-circle. A woman was laying next to one of the trees. Oleksiy rushed to the woman's side. The woman was alive, but she looked very poorly. Her fair hair was laying on top of most of her face and she was wrapped up in a warm coat. The little girl sat down beside her mother.

"She needs help. Please help her," the girl begged.

"She's got a fever," Oleksiy said whilst touching the woman's forehead and noticing that it was very hot. "We should take her to a hospital."

"Will she be all right?"

"I hope so," Oleksiy said optimistically, even though he did not know if the illness was serious or not.

He tried to pick the woman up, but all of a sudden she swung her eyes open and grabbed him by the collar. This startled Oleksiy and almost made him jump back.

"It's ok," he said, "I'm here to help you."

The woman continued looking at him for a few more seconds and then loosened her grasp of his collar and closed her eyes. Oleksiy picked her up in his arms and was ready to carry her back to the settlement. He began heading back through the forest path, with the girl walking by his side and Max on the other side.

"What's your name?" Oleksiy asked the little girl as they continued walking.

"Alina. And my mum's name is Maria. What's yours?"

"Oleksiy."

"I knew a boy in school who had that name too."

"Where do you and your mum live? How did you end up here in the woods?"

"We walked for 3 days from Bucha. Lots of bad soldiers there. They killed many people. They killed my dad. They also killed Georgiy. He was helping us."

Oleksiy could see that Alina was very sad when talking about this topic. She and her mother were in the occupied territory for some time and must've seen a lot of horrible things. For a small child like this to lose her father no doubt was traumatizing. Oleksiy realised that her pain must've been even worse than the pain he felt when his father died in the Donbas.

"Everything will be ok now," he said to Alina after a few seconds of thought. "There are no Russian soldiers here, so they won't hurt you here."

"Did they try to come here too?"

"They were here, yes. Our soldiers forced them out of here a day or two ago. They won't come back."

Alina nodded, showing that she understood everything. They continued along the path for some time. Oleksiy could roughly remember the direction he and Max came from and kept backtracking. His arms were getting a bit sore now as he was still carrying Maria in his arms. Having a supply bag hanging on his back too was making him feel somewhat exhausted. Nevertheless, he pressed on and intended to get Maria some medical help.

After a few more minutes, they could see the end of the woods ahead and some houses just beyond. The path seemed a lot longer on the way back, but they finally made it. Now they needed to find someone who could take Maria and Alina to a hospital.

25th of March
Mykolaiv

With a tray full of food, Solomiya entered the room where Zlata was. Solomiya spent many hours the last two days with the girl, trying to tend to all her needs and making sure she continued recovering. Zlata was very distressed the entire time, frequently looking at where her left arm used to be, trying to get used to it, and also occasionally asking if her parents were ok.

Solomiya set the tray of food down next to the girl's bed and sat down on a chair beside it. Zlata looked at the tray and grabbed a bowl with soup that was in it and then a piece of bread too. After two days of barely eating, it seemed Zlata's appetite had returned. To Solomiya this looked like a positive sign.

"Let me know if there's anything else you'd like me to bring," Solomiya spoke, trying to start a conversation.

"I'm fine, thank you. This stuff is good enough."

"Do you want me to put something on a TV for you?"

"No, that's ok. I don't really have an interest to watch anything. I don't watch much TV anyway."

"What do you like to do then?"

"I like to read about interesting things online. Things about animals for example, especially dinosaurs. I also like to read about planets and about countries and cultures too."

"Wow! You have a lot of passion for learning new things."

"It's very interesting. The world is so huge and has so much in it."

"Is there a country or a city that you want to visit the most then?"

Zlata thought for a moment. The question seemed to have intrigued her.

"You know, it's hard to pick just one place, because I want to see so many places, like Venice, Paris, Egypt, or even Japan."

"Your dreams will come true, dear," Solomiya encouraged her. "This war will end and you will see all those places. There will be better times ahead."

Zlata lowered her gaze and stopped eating. By the looks of it, it was very difficult for her to accept the reality and to see what her life turned into. Her mind was likely still in a state of shock and trying gradually to adjust to the events that were happening.

"Solomiya, can you please tell me the truth?" Zlata spoke and looked directly into Solomiya's eyes.

"About what, dear?"

"What happened to my mum and dad? Are they still alive?"

Solomiya was speechless and did not know what to say, and she could tell that Zlata was reading her emotions on her face.

"They're dead, aren't they?" Zlata asked in a half-crying voice.

Solomiya stayed silent, not wanting to make this news sound any more sorrowful than it was already. Zlata's eyes filled with tears and she began to cry. Solomiya put her arms around the child and brought her closer to herself. Zlata burrowed her face into Solomiya's shoulder and kept crying. Her right hand was clutching onto Solomiya's arm, as if she was afraid to lose Solomiya too.

Zlata cried non-stop for almost half an hour, until eventually she got sapped off her energy and went quiet. She had no more tears to cry. She was merely leaning her head sideways into Solomiya's chest and staring vacantly at the wall ahead. Solomiya kept silent and simply continued holding the girl tenderly and giving her all the warmth that she needed in that moment.

"Solomiya, have you lost anyone because of this war too?"

The girl's question startled Solomiya. It was so sudden and so direct. Solomiya did not see a reason to withhold any information. She was comfortable sharing personal details with Zlata and to build a closer bond with her.

"I lost my beloved man Tymur. I've been in pain ever since. He was everything to me – my rock, my world. And now he's gone forever and left me by myself, and I don't know what to do anymore. I feel like I've been thrown into a violent sea storm and now have to somehow find my way back on land."

Zlata raised her head and gazed Solomiya in the eyes. What Solomiya said touched the little girl as she could relate to the same emotional state of loss.

"Did he die while fighting the enemy?" she then asked.

"Yes, in the first few days of the invasion."

"Then he's a hero. He died so that you and I can live."

Solomiya nodded in agreement. She felt like tears were about to fall from her eyes, but she tried her best to stop them. She did not want to show herself being emotionally weak in front of the girl, but it was very hard.

"We'll stick together, ok? You have me and I have you," Solomiya suggested to the girl.

"Thank you," Zlata appreciated the suggestion.

A thunderous noise suddenly came from outside. A missile landed somewhere in the distance. Solomiya and Zlata both turned in the direction the noise came from. Then another impact was heard, closer this time. Zlata looked very scared, so Solomiya stood up and embraced her tightly, making sure to cover her fully in case anything fell on her.

Suddenly a third strike occurred, landing somewhere right next to the hospital. It shook the building violently. The shockwave shattered all the windows in the room, causing Zlata to shriek in terror. The windows were all barricaded and so none of the shards from broken windows could get into the room. Despite that, it was still a terrifying sound. Solomiya felt her heart beating at an alarming speed. She was expecting another missile to hit the hospital building directly and braced herself for any falling debris.

To their relief, there were no more blasts. They waited for another minute, but it was still quiet. Solomiya released Zlata but could still see Zlata shaking in fear. The little girl was traumatized. The shock from a bomb landing in her apartment, killing her parents and leaving her disabled continued being there and she was getting anxious over any loud noise.

"Solomiya, why do they want to kill us? Why?" Zlata asked in a trembling voice.

"Because they are not thinking straight. They are sick in the head and confused. People like that should be pitied," Solomiya replied in a heat of a moment, although she wasn't sure herself of the answer to the girl's question.

Zlata did not know what to say. She just agreed with Solomiya's response and then lay her head down on the bed.

"Get some rest now, ok? I won't be far and will keep checking up on you," Solomiya said after a short pause and got up from her chair.

"Ok, I will. Thank you for everything, Solomiya. You are very kind."

Solomiya merely smiled back and then headed out of the room. Once in the corridor, she wanted to check if everyone else was fine after the bombardment that had just occurred outside. A few nurses were hastily moving in the corridors and everyone continued working and helping the patients. It seemed that most hospital staff was used to this by now. The senior nurse, Vira, was passing by at that moment and stopped by Solomiya's side.

"How's Zlata doing? Has she eaten anything?"

"Yes, her appetite is returning. She's very vulnerable emotionally though. She figured out that her parents perished in the bombing."

"Poor thing. She would've had to find that out sooner or later. Please watch her closely, ok? Once she starts recovering, we might need your help with the wounded again. We keep getting more of them each day."

"Ok, I understand. May I ask one more thing whilst you're here?" Solomiya had an idea and she really wanted to find out what Vira would say.

"Of course. What would you like to ask?"

"Since Zlata has no-one to live with once she's discharged, I'd like to take care of her myself. I'd like for her to live with me. She needs all the love and support she can get."

"Hmm, if you are really sure about this, Solomiya, we can try to arrange that. You'll need to sign a few official papers and we'll need to get higher management to approve this. It could take a few days."

"I understand."

Vira then continued with her duties. Solomiya checked a few other wards to make sure everything was in order and nobody needed any help and then headed back to the room Zlata was in to watch over her. She knew it was the right decision to have Zlata come to live with her after being discharged. She felt it in her heart. Zlata needed someone dear nearby to help her recover emotionally, and Solomiya knew that she too needed someone dear nearby, someone she could care for.

27th of March
Kharkiv

Ksenia, Olesya and Vadym were gathered in the shelter, having a cup of tea. There was a lot of shelling happening in Kharkiv the last few days, so they had to spend a lot of their time in the shelter. Food was starting to run low again.

"We really need to leave the city as soon as possible. They'll bury us under the rubble if we don't," Olesya brought up the same topic they've been discussing for days now.

"Trouble is finding a suitable time when they're not dropping missiles on our heads. It will be dangerous," Vadym pointed out, "but I agree with you. We can't stay here forever."

Ksenia continued listening to them both discussing it for a minute and then went over to a small cabinet with some books. She searched around the books until she found the map of the country. It was still in a fairly good condition, so she took it with herself, walked over to Olesya and Vadym, and set down the map on the table in front of them.

"Let's begin planning our road," she suggested.

"Yes, we should've been doing that earlier," Olesya agreed.

"Where would you suggest to go?" Vadym asked. "Kyiv is still not safe."

"My parents live in Vinnytsia," Ksenia replied. "That might be the best place for us to go for now."

Olesya and Vadym both went silent and seemed to had begun considering that idea. Ksenia knew that trying to drive out of Kharkiv was still dangerous at this time, but they needed to take action soon as their supplies were running out and the city continued getting attacked every day.

"All right," Vadym agreed, "let's decide on our trip. If the next couple of days prove to be relatively safe, we can begin driving out of the city then."

"We could stop in Poltava," Ksenia suggested and pointed on the map. "It's a bit safer there and we'll be able to buy some more food for the road."

"Good idea," Vadym acknowledged. "We might need to spend the night there before proceeding further."

The three of them kept looking at the map after having decided the first stage of the journey. Vadym continued:

"Since the area around Kyiv is still dangerous, I suggest we do not go that way. I think from Poltava it would be better to go through Kremenchuk and then Kropyvnytskyi, and from there it's pretty much straight towards Vinnytsia. Those places are in the central parts of the country and far from all the fighting. I think it's the safest road for us."

Ksenia and Olesya continued inspecting the map and checking the route Vadym had suggested. It seemed like a reasonable road to take and neither of them had any objections. Once they concluded, Ksenia got up and walked over to the cabinet. She wanted to start deciding on what objects could be useful to take with them for the road. Olesya joined her half a minute later.

"I pray to God that everything goes fine this time," Olesya said before she began looking through a neighbouring cabinet. Her shoulder was noticeably better now, although she still tried not to overexert its joint.

"I hope for the same," responded Ksenia. "The most dangerous part is getting out of Kharkiv. Once we're beyond the city, it will be easier."

"Poor Anton. He had so much ahead of him still. His death was so unjust. I wish we hadn't tried to leave the city that day. He would've still been alive now."

"I know, dear, but we can't do anything about that now. Going through what we should've done will only make you feel worse."

"Yeah, perhaps you're right."

Olesya stopped looking in the cabinet and just sat down on the floor, her eyes were looking down. Ksenia stopped as well for a moment and turned to her friend. She could feel that Olesya was being tormented by thoughts.

"How are your nightmares by the way?" Ksenia asked. The two girls discussed this topic with each other a lot in the first two weeks of the invasion, but in the last few days they were bringing it up less and less.

"Not quite as frequent as before, but I still get them from time to time. Two nights ago I saw us all sitting in our apartment when some soldiers burst in through the front doors and began shooting at us. I woke up very sharply from that, feeling my heart pounding hard in my chest. Couldn't fall asleep for a full hour after that."

"I've been plagued by similar kinds of dreams," Ksenia admitted.

"I just hope all this ends soon. I can't bear losing anyone else dear to me. I won't survive it. If I lose my dad or you, my psyche will just break."

Ksenia shifted herself closer to her dear friend and gently put her hands on her shoulders.

"You will not lose me, Olesya. I'll be close by to always support you, just as you have always supported me over the years."

Olesya looked up at Ksenia and gave a feeble smile after hearing such compassionate words. She then gave Ksenia a tight hug. Olesya was in a lot of emotional pain. They all were. This pain could haunt them for a long time. There was no escaping it. The only thing they could do was to face it together and support each other.

28th of March
Mariupol

Danyil and Lera were in a shelter. The situation in Mariupol continued worsening exponentially. There was now fierce fighting happening within the city and some parts of the city had already been taken over by the enemy forces. It was inevitable that the city would fall under the enemy's control soon. And escaping it now was even harder and more dangerous than earlier in the month.

Danyil's hands had healed for the most part, but both he and Lera were in a terrible state. Water continued being scarce. They frequently found themselves thirsty, only having enough water to continue surviving, but not to feel their thirst fully quenched. Food was also rapidly declining. There was now none of it left in the shelter, and going out to get more was far too dangerous. Neither Danyil nor Lera had eaten anything this entire day and were both terribly hungry. Because of this, they were both feeling low on energy and unwilling to do anything other than lie on their beds and talk. There were fewer other people in the shelter now too. Only a handful of others remained. Most must have either been killed or had tried to flee the city. Death of a loved one or an acquaintance became a regular occurrence for many.

"I have failed us, Lera," Danyil said bitterly whilst laying on his back and staring at a blank ceiling above him.

"No, you haven't."

"I have. I promised mum and dad that I'd look after you. I tried getting us out of the city, but it all led to nothing. I am useless."

"Don't say that! You are the best brother anyone could ever ask for!"

"Our only choice, if we want to stay alive, is to evacuate to Russia."

"No! This is not a choice! How can we trust them to treat us with any dignity? If I'm going to die, I'd rather die on my home soil, and not on the territory of the enemy."

Danyil desperately wanted to do everything possible so that his sister would stay alive and be out of this hell. There was no certainty with any of the choice. To stay here and die, to try fleeing and die, or to evacuate to the territory of the enemy and get treated with humiliation?

Thunderous noises of shelling were heard coming from outside again. It sounded like the missiles landed very close. Danyil and Lera were already used to this discordant sound. Hearing bombardment on a daily basis became a normality. Sounds of shelling were nothing more than just background noise at this point. And lately, because of street fighting happening, they began hearing booming noises of tank gunfire too. It only added to the disharmonic symphony of impending doom.

For a brief moment both of them heard the shelter door opening, making all the noises from outside louder for a fraction of a second, until the door was closed again. Someone just came into the shelter. Perhaps one of the other people had returned. The footsteps sounded heavy though. Danyil couldn't see who it was as the room they were staying in was not directly facing the shelter entrance. They then heard a harsh masculine voice.

"Everybody out!"

Both Danyil and Lera sharply rose from their beds, their hearts pounding in terror.

"It's one of them," Lera said quietly so only her brother could hear. "They're already here."

"Hide," Danyil uttered to her and got up onto his feet.

They could now hear the voices of other shelter dwellers next door, talking to the man that just walked in. Danyil and Lera listened in and could make out some words. They were now sure that the man that entered was a Russian soldier. The other people in the shelter began begging for the man to have some mercy, but their voices were quickly silenced by deafening gunfire. Danyil could see his sister in absolute terror. Her eyes were reflecting a sense of despondency even more now than before. The two of them scurried towards a nearby cabinet and hid behind it, hoping that the intruder would just leave.

"Come out now! I know you're here!" the man yelled out loud and then entered the room they were in.

Danyil could tell that the man was still standing at the doorway and it was not possible to see the other side of the cabinet from there. So long as the man did not move any further in, he would not see them.

A burst of gunfire came suddenly, making Lera abruptly gasp out loud. The intruder was clearly trying to scare them, and after Lera's gasp, there was no doubt that he had heard them.

"Come out nicely and I won't shoot you," he said a second later.

"He knows we're here," Lera whispered to Danyil with tears in her eyes.

Danyil put a finger to his lips to gesture for her to be quiet and then listened in to the man's actions. Footsteps resumed, now coming closer to them. Louder and louder with each step. He was approaching.

"You think I'm stupid?" he appeared in front of them from around the cabinet all of a sudden.

Before either Danyil or Lera could react, the enemy soldier grabbed Danyil by the shoulder with one of his hands and pulled him roughly. On a normal day Danyil would've managed to withstand such pull, but because he was hungry and sapped off energy, he felt his legs give way and he fell face forward to the floor.

When he turned to look up at the man, he saw the man grabbing and pushing Lera onto the ground too. She was now crying in full and asking him to stop. Danyil tried to get back up onto his feet and to protect his sister, but the soldier walked up to him and kicked him hard in the chest, sending him tumbling backwards with force.

"No! Leave my brother alone!" Lera shouted and grabbed the soldier by the right leg with both of her hands, trying her best to stop him from moving.

The soldier turned his head towards her with an annoyed expression on the face and struck her on the back with the butt of his rifle. She cried from the sharp pain and let go off his leg whilst still crawling on the floor.

Danyil looked hastily around, hoping to use something to fight back against the cruel and sadistic invader. His eyes stopped on something. A shovel! He reached out and grabbed it tightly with both hands. A bout of strength came to him and he rose up. The soldier was still looking down at Lera and began turning in Danyil's direction. Danyil reacted swiftly and swung with the shovel at the intruder, striking him directly in the face.

The strike was powerful enough to cause the Russian soldier to drop his rifle and fall onto the ground. He was not out of his senses, however, and tried to get back up. Danyil swung with the shovel again, this time overhead, and forcefully brought it down on the soldier's head. In the heat of the moment, he did not want to leave things to chance, so he picked up the intruder's rifle and without hesitance fired several shots at him.

Harsh, ear-bursting sounds of gunfire came and the intruder was laying motionless on the floor, a puddle of blood beginning to form under him. Danyil continued breathing fast and hard, clutching onto the gun and aiming it at the Russian soldier's corpse, preparing to shoot in case the soldier got back up to continue hurting him or his sister.

Half a minute passed. Danyil continued staring. The corpse continued laying still. Danyil dropped the gun and fell to his knees, still in shock. He looked over towards his sister to see if she was fine. She was sitting on the floor, shifting her shocked eyes from the soldier's corpse to Danyil and then back, utter terror on her face.

"He's dead," Danyil murmured finally. "I killed the bastard."

Lera crawled over to her brother's side and grabbed him by the right arm. She was shaken and needed some comfort. Danyil couldn't get a hold of himself either. The sense of alarm inside of him persisted and he kept thinking that another soldier would enter the shelter at any moment now.

Lera continued holding onto his arm and squeezing it hard, her forehead was resting on his shoulder and he could hear her sobbing. He brought his other arm around her and gave her a hug. He never killed anyone before, not until now. It was still hard to accept that he had just murdered another person, but he did not feel guilty. He knew there was no other way. Had he not killed this man, the man would've killed him and his sister. It was kill or be killed.

"We should go to another shelter," Danyil said after a couple of more minutes. "It's no longer safe in this one."

Chapter 9

Solomiya was having an early morning walk through the city. She finally got a day off after working non-stop for two weeks. Having to work so much was burning her out internally and she had no energy on anything else outside of work. Although the last few days she found to be easier and less stressful as she got to spend a lot of time with Zlata. With Zlata making a fast recovery, Solomiya felt more positive and more hopeful. She felt that perhaps things were beginning to slowly improve. The weather also bit by bit started getting warmer as the spring was finally arriving.

It was still rather dangerous to be outside of home, but Solomiya really needed fresh air. After having spent so many hours each day lately inside an overcrowded hospital with stuffy air, she needed to spend some time on her day off to walk around and enjoy the sunshine. There were a few other people on the streets too, though not like on a normal day during a time of peace. Although some people were trying to get on with their lives and feel some sense of normality, many others were still scared and remained indoors.

Suddenly the all-too-familiar sound of a missile came from the distance. Solomiya turned in the direction of the sound but didn't see anything. A moment later she heard an explosion somewhere nearby and she immediately understood that the enemy was bombing the city again. She looked around in a panic to try and get herself to safety of a shelter somewhere, but then she stopped as another thought struck her. The place that just got hit would likely have many people needing help, and her nature was to always help others if it was within her ability. She could not run away and look out only for her own life at a time like this. Every cell in her body was resisting this action. So instead of seeking safety, she began looking for where the missile landed.

A few other people on the street were heading in the direction of the explosion, so she followed them. A few more turns around street corners and she finally saw it. It was the regional administration building. Solomiya widened her eyes in shock when she saw what happened to it. An immense see-through hole was made in the middle of the building due to the explosion, as though someone erased a section of the building completely or carved it out with a giant knife. Fires were burning all around the newly-made hole, and mountains of debris were formed at the foot of the building.

Solomiya put her hands to her mouth out of shock, trying to take in the scene but struggling to accept it. The barbaric nature of this attack was incomprehensible. This was a civilian building. It was not a military base or a storage of military equipment. It was a regular office building for the state administration where ordinary civilians came to work.

She continued walking towards the scene. Groups of people were now gathered some distance away from it. There were no rescue services at the scene yet, but they were likely already on the way.

"Don't get so close, lady. Some parts of the building are still collapsing," a nearby man warned her.

Solomiya didn't realise that she was getting quite close to the building, so she took a few steps back as per the man's advice and waited. She was determined to stay at the scene and provide care and help for any wounded, even on her day off. Saving lives was not just a job to her. It was at the core of who she was.

30ᵗʰ of March
Somewhere near Kherson

Taras and Roman had everything prepared and ready for execution of their plan. The breakout was going to occur tonight, and there was only one chance to get it right. They along with every other prisoner were in the same tiny room where they had been forced to spend most hours of their day. It was night time already and Taras was sure that only a small handful of Russian soldiers were awake in the whole building and not all of those who were awake were nearby.

"Here, you'll need it," Roman handed Taras a small wooden fragment of a broken chair leg. It was only about the size of a grown man's open palm, but it was sharp and useful for close-range attacks. Roman also still had his shard of glass, which he kept himself.

"Let's begin," Taras announced to his friend.

Roman nodded and signalled to the other prisoners that things were about to get hectic. One of the prisoners, who had a scab-covered injury on one arm after one of the beatings he received from Russian soldiers, began digging in his wound and making it bleed. When the blood began to flow, he started wiping it on his clothes and then also on his face.

Taras edged closer to the only door in the room and knocked on it. The Russian soldiers on the other side weren't always willing to respond to requests from the prisoners. Most times they pitilessly ignored them. However, this night, Taras knew on night watch were two relatively new guys, Petrov and Babanin, and they were likely to respond.

Just as he had predicted, a few seconds later the door was unlocked and then swung open. Petrov and Babanin were standing there with rifles at the ready.

"You better have a good reason to disturb us in the middle of the night," Petrov said threateningly.

"One of us is heavily bleeding. His wound got worse," Taras said and pointed at the prisoner who had wiped blood all over himself a minute ago.

The two Russian soldiers switched on the lights in the room and looked carefully at the prisoner Taras was pointing at.

"What the hell, man?" Babanin commented out loud.

"You need to give him a medical treatment," Taras said.

"We'll do whatever the hell we choose to do, so shut your mouth," Petrov silenced him. He then pointed his skinny finger at the bloodied prisoner and said, "You there, come over here."

The prisoner listened and began crawling closer to the door. Smears of blood were left all over the floor after him. Just as he reached the door, he fell fully to the floor. Petrov crouched down to take a closer look at the prisoner's wound. This was the moment Taras had been waiting for. Now that Petrov was crouching down next to him, Taras took out the broken fragment of a chair leg and in a swift motion stabbed it in the side of Petrov's neck, bringing an instant death to the Russian soldier.

Roman was ready, and once Taras did his move, Roman leapt into the doorway where Babanin was standing and sliced his throat with the glass shard. The Russian soldier did not have the time to realise what had just happened, but he pointed his weapon at Roman and prepared to fire. Roman grabbed the end of the rifle and forced it to point up. A couple of bullets were fired until the enemy soldier collapsed dead from the mortal wound on his throat.

"Damn it! The others must've woken up now!" Taras said with annoyance.

"Then we need to act quickly," Roman uttered and grabbed the fallen soldier's assault rifle.

Taras took the rifle of the other soldier and gave a handgun to another prisoner. The prisoners started to quickly exit the room into the main hall, led by Taras and Roman. The lights in the main hall were switched off, but the light in the corridor ahead went on. Taras remembered that the Russian soldiers usually slept in a few rooms down that corridor, so he already knew where they would be coming from.

Everyone took hiding spots and cover within the main hallway and waited. They only had a few firing weapons between them and hence were still outgunned. A few seconds had passed and Taras could see silhouettes of Russian soldiers coming down the corridor. He aimed with the rifle, waited for them to get a bit closer, and then opened fire. A few of the soldiers were neatly lined up as they were running down the corridor, so he managed to hit several of them at once, killing two within moments.

The surviving soldiers returned fire and a dangerous gunfight began in the building. Within moments the levels of noise in the building rose up tremendously. Loud gunfire, yelling, glass shattering, and things falling onto the floor. There was chaos, but Russian soldiers remained hidden in the doorways along each side of the corridor, refusing to enter the main hallway and to get themselves exposed.

A peculiar sound then came of something metallic bouncing along the floor. Taras peeked out to see what it was and saw with fear in his eyes that it was a grenade.

"Take cover!" he growled loudly and hid behind a protrusion in a wall.

The grenade exploded with a deafening noise. A few of the prisoners weren't fast enough to move out of its vicinity and got killed either by the explosion or the shrapnel that flew out. Taras got fed up and decided to push on forward. He ran out of cover and sprinted in the direction of the corridor. Once he spotted Russian soldiers preparing to fire, he slid into the nearby cover just in time. Now that he was in a better position, he could take out a few more ruscists. And just as he expected, he managed to deliver a few well-placed shots to take out two more soldiers in the corridor.

This created an opening, allowing other prisoners to swarm into the corridor and attack the remaining enemy soldiers. A huge scuffle broke out in the corridor, with screams and aggressive yelling. Sprays of blood came from the mass of punching and kicking bodies and landed on the nearby walls. All the hatred the prisoners felt for their captors during these days had boiled over and erupted into frightening acts of violence. All the humiliation they endured only made them more relentless and willing to treat the enemy as nothing more than wild animals that should be put down by any means necessary.

When the fighting was over, the corridor looked like a slaughterhouse. Not a single Russian soldier remained alive. A few of the prisoners also perished, several others were injured. Taras knew the fighting during their breakout would be bloody and violent, but he did not expect the level of carnage that he was looking at in that instant. It was the harshest, most inhumane scene of violence he had ever seen in his life.

"We got them all!" Roman walked up to Taras whilst wiping droplets of blood off his face.

"How many of ours died?"

"Quite a few unfortunately."

Taras asked for everyone to gather in the main hallway and looked around to see who survived. Aside from him and Roman, there were nine other survivors, which meant that about half of the prisoners had perished in the fighting. Both of the female prisoners were among the fallen too. Taras felt particularly sorry for them as they had endured the worst humiliation of all during these days.

"So, what now?" one of the prisoners asked Taras and Roman.

"Before we do anything else, we should first pay respects to our fallen brothers and sisters," Taras expressed out loud so that everyone could hear him clearly.

All of the prisoners agreed. They gathered the dead bodies of the other fallen prisoners in one place. Then they all stood in a circle around their fallen brothers and sisters and slowly got down on one knee. Taras lowered his head and closed his eyes. The others did the same. For a few seconds they maintained silence, thanking those who died for their sacrifice and swearing to not rest until the enemy was beaten in the whole of Ukraine.

"Slava Ukraini!" Taras then said, the words meaning 'Glory to Ukraine'.

"Heroyam slava!" everyone responded, meaning 'Glory to the heroes'.

When they were done, they all searched around the rooms where their captors were spending time for any useful weapons, supplies and food rations. After that they headed outside to the front of the building where three military cars were located.

"Here's what we're going to do from here on," Taras announced. "Our enemy has taken Kherson, but Mykolaiv is still ours. I'd like two or three of us to deliver a message to those in Mykolaiv. It will be a dangerous journey, however. Any volunteers?"

"I'll go," Roman stepped forward. Two others did too.

"What about the rest of us?" asked another prisoner.

"The rest of us will go to Kherson. We're going to encourage partisan activities there. No doubt many of our people are trapped there and would be willing to act to make life of the occupiers more difficult. If anyone is unwilling to do that, please say so now and begone."

There was silence. Every person in their group kept nodding and it seemed they all shared the same sentiments as Taras. They all wanted to return their city back from the enemy's grasp. Roman then walked over to Taras to get more details of what message to deliver to those in Mykolaiv.

"Tell them about the planned partisan activities in Kherson. We're going to try and coordinate it all with them so that it will be easier for them to retake the city down the line."

"Are you sure this will work?"

"No, but what else are we to do? We have to fight," Taras said with a hint of melancholy in his voice and then continued, "Oh and can I ask you for one more thing?"

"Anything."

"When you get to Mykolaiv, please find a way to get on the line with my wife, Viktoria Shulga, and tell her that I'm alive and fine. I need for her to know that."

"It will be done, Taras. I'll make sure of that."

"Thank you, Roman. I don't know when I'll see you next, but go safely. You might want to put on some Russian uniforms whilst you're still sneaking through the occupied territories. Take one of the vehicles with you too."

"Good idea."

"And now to finalise here," Taras proclaimed and turned towards the building, "we're going to burn it down so that nobody finds out about our escape."

Danyil and Lera were moving through a destroyed street as carefully as they could, constantly looking around for signs of danger. Every noise was startling them, regardless of whether it sounded close or far away. They were shaken after all these days, but they knew they had to move on for their own survival.

The street looked macabre, as though hell itself had absorbed it into its domain. The cars and the trees were on fire, with black plumes of smoke coming. A sickening smell of burnt rubber was emanating from the blazing cars. Even bigger plumes of smoke were coming from the buildings, or what was left of them. Not a single building in the vicinity was untouched. Each one was beaten into a state of infirmity by persistent missile fire that occurred over the last few weeks. The road was full of large dents from the missile impacts and heaps of debris. Some parts of the road were entirely buried under mountains of rubble and remains of the buildings that were smitten from existence.

They walked further and could see more devastation everywhere, with each step making them feel that they were venturing deeper into the mouth of hell. Decaying dead bodies were laying scattered all over the road ahead. Many were surrounded by puddles of blood. Torn individual limbs could also be seen left lying in some places, covered in blood and dirt. A couple of dishevelled stray dogs with a hollow gaze were feeding on one of the corpses, trying to satiate their hunger. The sight of that made both Danyil and Lera feel sick to their stomachs.

"Danyil, are you sure this is the right way? I feel like we're only getting closer to all the fighting," Lera expressed her inner doubts.

"Yes. We're almost there," Danyil replied with certainty.

"Do you think this guy is trustworthy? He won't just deliver us to the Russians, will he?"

"I don't know, but we have to do something to get out of here. If we don't act now, we'll end up just like all these people you see here."

Danyil had found a man a day earlier who was taking civilians out of Mariupol, and they were meant to meet him in a location close by. Danyil did not know if this would work out or if it would lead them to more problems, but after being attacked in their shelter, it became clear that sitting quietly in a shelter was no longer a good option for surviving this hell. They understood now that taking a risk and dying on the road was a better option than staying and getting buried in the shelter under mountains of rubble from destroyed buildings.

More distant explosions were heard, followed by sounds of tanks firing. Despite how unnerving all these sounds were, Danyil and Lera continued. They barely ate the last two days, having to resort mostly to some remains of mouldy bread that they had found.

They made a turn in the road into a narrow alleyway that was filled with broken glass and pieces of scrap metal, and then from that alleyway they stepped into another street that was in a similar condition as the one before. Up ahead they could see a light grey van and a group of people next to it.

"That's the place. He said he'll be by a grey van," Danyil said with a sense of relief.

"Why…" Lera began, "why are there soldiers there?"

Danyil looked closer. The man, Yaroslav, whom they were supposed to meet, was there, but he was in an altercation with three Russian soldiers. The soldiers didn't appear to be attacking anyone, but they were demanding something. Danyil moved his right hand behind his back to where he kept a handgun in his trousers. The Russian soldier that he had to kill in self-defence two days ago had it on him and Danyil was now carrying it in case he had to defend his sister or himself again.

When they got nearer, they could hear the argument better. The Russian soldiers were trying to stop Yaroslav from evacuating a small group of civilians.

"But I've got a permission," Yaroslav was saying to them. "I've been helping to evacuate the civilians for the last two weeks."

"Times have changed. They're not going anywhere, and neither are you," one of the soldiers stated firmly.

"Why don't you contact the guys at the checkpoint and they'll tell you?"

"We're not contacting anyone. Everyone, out of the van!"

There were about a dozen of people crammed inside the van, mainly women and children. They were too scared to exit the van. Nobody trusted the Russian soldiers and wanted to just peacefully leave the city.

"I said – out!" the Russian soldier shouted on top of his voice and fired a couple of rounds into the air from his rifle in an attempt to scare the people inside the van to do what he said.

Danyil was furious upon seeing this and knew that this was their last chance to escape. He could not allow those degenerates to get in the way, so in a blink of an eye he took out a handgun that he was carrying, directed it at the yelling soldier and shot him at a point blank range. A sudden and loud sound from the gunshot made everyone else jump in fear. A burst of blood sprayed from the murdered soldier's head back at the two others. Danyil did not wait for a reaction. He then aimed the gun at the next soldier and fired it mercilessly, taking the enemy down within a second. The third soldier was already tackling him when he attempted to aim and the two of them began to wrestle.

The soldier was a large and stout man and Danyil found himself getting pushed back, barely keeping his balance. Lera and Yaroslav tried to grab onto the soldier and pull him back, but with one sharp swing of his arm, he threw them backwards. The gunfire alerted a few other enemy soldiers to the location, who could now be seen coming from down the street.

"Lera, get out of here!" Danyil shouted whilst trying his best to overpower the large soldier, "Yaroslav, take her and go!"

"Come on, we must go now," Yaroslav told Lera as he helped her up from the ground.

"No, I'm not leaving my brother!"

"Go!" Danyil yelled as he and the Russian soldier fell onto the ground and continued their fierce fight there.

Yaroslav grabbed Lera and pulled her into the van. Danyil was feeling his strength dissipating while the Russian soldier was trying to pin him down on the ground, but he refused to give in until his sister was safely away from this place. The other soldiers were already near and could see what was happening. Danyil heard the engine of the van come on and it beginning to hastily drive off with a screech of the wheels.

When it drove out of sight, Danyil felt a mild sense of relief and stopped resisting. There was no more reason to continue wasting his inner energy. He knew he was about to be caught and he was ready to accept that. The soldier noticed that and loosened his grip as well, although he continued to pin Danyil to the ground. A group of other Russian soldiers arrived at the scene.

"What happened?" one of them asked.

"Take this troublemaker away. I think we'll need to teach him some manners."

The next thing Danyil saw was a fist rapidly approaching his face and knocking his senses out.

Lera was crying and screaming her brother's name whilst at the back of the van as it sped through the ravaged street that was littered with bricks and corpses. She kept looking through the tiny back window even after they cleared the area and Danyil was no longer in sight. She could feel her heart getting heavier and heavier with each moment.

When reality finally sunk in and she understood that she could not change what just happened, she slumped down to the floor of the van and lay down in a foetal position. She could not think about anything anymore. Her worst fears of losing her brother had just come true. Her mind went numb and she no longer cared what would happen to her. She just wished she would die in peace and escape this pain once and for all.

31st of March
Outskirts of Kyiv

Oleksiy was sitting at the back of a small truck along with a few other men. They were part of a backup team, coming to help out soldiers at the frontline. Oleksiy was very nervous. He was going into an active warzone, and although the enemy was on a retreat in the village he was being sent to, it was still highly dangerous as the Russian forces kept regularly shelling the areas they retreated from.

He had to leave Max temporarily in the care of a few very kind people in one of the villages where he was helping out. He knew he won't see Max for a few days. He was getting attached to his new canine friend. With Dmytro not being around anymore, Oleksiy's main company was Max. He still hadn't the chance to return and check up on Dmytro, neither did he get to check on Maria and Alina after helping them. He wanted for everyone to recover and get better and for life to return to normal again. He wished this war would end as soon as possible.

"We're here," one of the soldiers said as the truck came to a stop.

Oleksiy followed the others as they all jumped out of the truck. A few other trucks were coming in, also filled with soldiers and volunteers. Each one was armed with a rifle. Oleksiy had a chance to practice shooting a bit in the last few days and was getting better. He was starting to feel more confident in case he needed to shoot at something, but he could still not overpower the general feeling of anxiety, the idea that danger was very close and that powerful war machines were nearby which could kill him in one shot and leave nothing but a bloodstain behind.

"They've fled already," the commander of one of the units already present in that village said. "But a few of them that didn't manage to escape in time could still be hiding around the place. I'd like you all to scout the area and make sure it's clear."

Oleksiy was partially relieved. Even though it was still dangerous and some enemy soldiers could be around, at least the bulk of the force was gone from the village and Ukrainian troops had control there.

The next few hours were long and tiring. Oleksiy lost his sense of direction after walking through so many similar-looking streets together with a handful of other soldiers. Many of the streets had mangled and charred corpses of soldiers lying in places. It was evident from fresh puddles of blood and smoking buildings that the fighting there was very recent. Only a few hours ago these corpses were people, and now there was no more life in them. Oleksiy tried his best not to linger his gaze on any of the dead bodies as he knew he'd accidentally see something that could haunt him forever. He just made sure to stick with the others in his group and to check the area for signs of enemy soldiers.

Overtime they managed to find two wounded Russian soldiers who surrendered as soon as they were found. The Russian soldiers were fearful and admitted that they were left behind by their squads as those fled in a hurry from the area. The sense of hurry of the fleeing enemy troops was noticeable also in the fact that they simply abandoned many of their military vehicles. Most of those vehicles were still in a good condition but were either out of fuel or stuck somewhere in the road.

By late afternoon, the area was declared to be secure. Many civilians living in this village were already outside, celebrating the liberation of the village from the notorious "Russian World". Oleksiy saw very touching scenes of how the civilians were greeting the Ukrainian soldiers, hugging them, talking to them and offering them food that they had at home. They all had to endure living under the occupation of the enemy forces for a whole month, and now they were finally free and their defenders were here to protect them. Even though the war was not yet over, they were safe now as the enemy was far away.

A few more soldiers arrived later in the day. Some of them had family members in this village whom they had not seen all month because of the enemy occupation. Oleksiy saw one soldier being very emotional and hugging his mother; another one was hugging his wife and two of his small children with tears in the eyes, relieved that they were unharmed.

Seeing all this was beautiful and heart-warming. After so much adversity and so much pain, good things began to happen. Oleksiy wished he would see his family again very soon too. He hoped the war would end quickly and his mother and sister would be back in Kyiv again. He missed them greatly. Even despite speaking with them on the phone every day, he missed having them near in person.

It seemed like a miracle to Lera that they managed to get out of Mariupol. Each time they came across a checkpoint, she expected the worst, but they were allowed through every single time. Now, a day and a half later, they finally made it to Zaporizhzhia, where Yaroslav used to transport the people before coming back to Mariupol for more.

Once they were near a bus stop, everyone began getting out of the van except for Lera. She remained seated against one of the walls, staring into space and lost in her thoughts. All life was drained from her. When everyone left the van, Yaroslav came closer and sat down opposite to her.

"How are you feeling?" he asked. "I know you're missing your brother and wish he was here."

Lera looked up at him but didn't say anything. Although he was trying to show some care and compassion, his words were barely even scratching the surface of what she was feeling. He continued:

"I think you really need some help. You're still a minor, and being all alone is dangerous."

"I have nowhere to go," Lera interrupted him. "I have nothing to live for either. My whole family has been taken away from me by those ruscists."

"You are still too young to be giving up. Here, take this card," he stretched out his hand with a card of a charity organisation. "This woman has been helping out people who have lost their families and homes. She lives in Vinnytsia."

"Vinnytsia is far away from here. I have no means to get there."

Yaroslav looked down and shook his head for a moment, thinking deeply about something. A few moments later he looked up again and began:

"Tell you what. I am not going to go back to Mariupol anymore. It's become too dangerous now and the city is about to fall. I had a deal with the guys at the checkpoints and paid them bribes to let me through. They were forthcoming as I have a Russian citizenship, so they decided not to bother me too much. But the ones occupying the city centre now will be a lot harder to convince. So, for your brother's sake, I'll take you to Vinnytsia. Just going to try and get a few more passengers and we'll set off in a few hours. How does that sound?"

"Thank you," Lera said and looked up from the floor at him again.

"Ok, good. It's settled then. I understand you're in pain. Mariupol was my home too, even though I was born in Russia. Of my 52 years on this Earth, I lived the last 35 years in Mariupol. And now that beautiful city is nothing but a bunch of ruins, destroyed by the people that were supposed to be my own brothers."

"They are monsters," Lera stated with hatred in her voice. "I can't see them as human beings anymore for everything they've done to us."

"I know and I understand your feelings about them. I really do. But please don't let this destroy your life. You have to move forward. But anyway, while we're waiting, let's go and get you something to eat. You look very feeble and need to get your strength up."

Chapter 10

2nd of April
Bucha

The Russian forces were retreating very rapidly from the area of Kyiv oblast. Oleksiy was helping the soldiers in their mission to reclaim previously occupied territories, to fortify defences there and to help out the local civilians. Over the past two days he found himself mostly on the road. It felt good to be part of the effort of liberating Ukrainian territories from the Russian forces. Even if he didn't do any active fighting himself, he knew that all the help given to the army and the civilians was useful. He felt hopeful in seeing the enemy retreating so quickly. *"Could the war be finally getting over?"* He kept thinking again and again.

The truck full of soldiers and volunteers where Oleksiy was now arrived in a part of Bucha. The occupiers had only left it very recently and the area was still getting secured. Oleksiy remembered that Maria and Alina, whom he found in the woods over a week ago, said that they travelled from Bucha and that the enemy soldiers killed many people here. He could now see the scale and intensity of the devastation incurred on Bucha with his own eyes and it was dreadful beyond his imagination.

The place was turned inside out. Broken roads, shattered buildings, destroyed military vehicles left in the middle of the streets, trash and building debris strewn everywhere. But this was not the worst of it. Oleksiy held his stare on several dead bodies lying in random places all along the road. Those did not look like military personnel. They were civilians. Innocent civilians were murdered and left to rot in the middle of the street.

The group Oleksiy was travelling with kept going further, and each new street they passed looked just as disturbing and ghastly as the last. A lot of the violence here looked deliberate.

"This…" one of the soldiers began as he stopped beside Oleksiy, "this is the worst I've seen so far."

"Yes, me too," Oleksiy stated whilst feeling nauseous. "What the hell did they do here?"

"Russian World. What else?"

Oleksiy was starting to feel unwell and homesick. The state of this place was scaring him and he was apprehensive about what else waited for him here and what other horrors he would see. He knew he had to be strong and continue helping, but this place was much worse than the others he'd seen after the occupiers were gone. Whatever he would see here, he knew it would haunt him forever and leave a permanent imprint in his mind.

2nd of April
Somewhere near Kropyvnytskyi

Vadym, Olesya and Ksenia were driving for the last few days and making regular stops in the larger settlements and cities. Within the next hour or so they would be reaching Kropyvnytskyi city. Ksenia was feeling a lot more relaxed as she believed the worst was behind them. They were out of Kharkiv safely and far from the frontline. Olesya was still tense, however, so Ksenia was sitting at the backseat of the car to keep her company and help her to feel calmer. Olesya was leaning on her shoulder for the last half an hour and sitting quietly.

They had all heard the news already about the retreat of the Russian forces near Kyiv and the northern parts of Ukraine. Those news were giving them hope and the anticipation of a possible end of this war in the near future.

"Maybe we'll end up returning to Kharkiv very soon," Ksenia said, feeling a little hopeful. "The Russian forces appear to be on the run already."

"Don't be too hasty," Vadym responded with some pessimism. "Even if they retreat from Kharkiv oblast, the city is still way too close to the border. They can continue shelling it for as long as the war continues."

"I guess it's best to stay somewhere safer for now then."

"Unfortunately nowhere in Ukraine is safe at the moment, but some places are a safer bet than others."

"I don't think anywhere is safe," Olesya spoke up at this point. "Russian authorities do not seem to care about any international agreements. If they feel like attacking any other country, they'll do it, and the rest of the world will just continue watching the injustices unfold and do very little to help."

"Let's wait and see," Vadym commented on what she said. "Some help is coming our way from other countries. It's just happening slowly. We need to stay strong and endure until there's enough support."

Ksenia thought about what both of them said. It was hard to know how the events would unfold and what could be done to stop this brutal invasion. Her thoughts were interrupted by something she saw up ahead. It was a vehicle laying on its side at one of the edges of the road, a grey van. Vadym was the first to speak.

"Something happened here."

"Shall we stop and see if anyone is still there? They might be needing help," Ksenia suggested.

"All right, but don't take too long. Whoever caused this van to tip over could still be around."

They stopped their car just behind the van. For a few seconds all three of them just looked ahead as if expecting someone to come out of the van. Then Vadym opened his car door and got out. Ksenia and Olesya followed suit.

"Shit!" Vadym exclaimed.

"What!?" Olesya reacted sharply.

"There are bullet holes on the side of this van. I didn't notice them from back there. It was being shot at."

"Does that mean Russian troops are in the area?" Ksenia asked with a sense of fear building up inside her.

"I hope not," replied Vadym and continued approaching the back of the van.

Ksenia looked around in all directions just to be sure it was safe. There were mainly fields stretching all around, so it was possible to see very far into the distance in every direction. She couldn't see anything suspicious. It was peaceful. Even the air felt calm, as though nothing even happened here.

Vadym pulled on one of the doors at the back of the van and got it opened. Ksenia walked closer and looked inside. What she saw shocked her to the very core. Several people were lying dead inside it and covered in blood. She could see the front windscreen of the van from the back and it was riddled with bullet holes and splashes of blood.

"I think I'm going to be sick," Ksenia said whilst feeling like a cold blade was bursting out of her stomach.

Olesya turned away in an instant and didn't even get any closer to the van to see inside it. Vadym continued looking, startled and depressed.

A feminine gasp came all of a sudden from the pile of people inside the van. All three of them swiftly turned towards the sound, utterly surprised.

"Someone's alive!" Ksenia exclaimed.

"Stay here," Vadym instructed and then climbed inside.

Another gasp came, followed by heavy breathing and pain grunts. Vadym moved a couple of corpses to the side and pulled out a young teenage girl. Her clothes were drenched in blood, but she didn't appear to have any serious injuries herself. The girl was in a state of shock and began crying gently.

"Are you hurt?" Vadym asked her as he pulled her out from the pile of corpses closer to the backdoors of the van and began checking her for any injuries.

"My head hurts," she admitted and sat up. "A helicopter appeared out of nowhere. It shot at us. The others got hit. It didn't get me as I was at the back."

"Hey, it will be ok, dear," Ksenia put her hand on the girl's shoulder and tried to calm her. "What is your name?"

"Lera."

"Where were you driving from, Lera?"

"Zaporizhzhia. Well, Mariupol actually. We stopped at Zaporizhzhia and then got some more passengers and continued further to get to Vinnytsia."

Ksenia was both shocked and amazed that this brave girl managed to get out of Mariupol, a place that everyone heard was going through hell.

"Well, we're going to Vinnytsia too. You should come with us. It will be safer."

"First we should get her some medical help," Vadym pointed out. "She was lucky not to get shot, but she is still concussed from the van toppling over."

"How far is it to Kropyvnytskyi?"

"Perhaps around 40 minutes or so. Let's make haste. The sooner we get there, the sooner we can find a hospital and get her some medical help."

Lera got out of the van but struggled to walk by herself, so Ksenia kept holding and supporting her. Olesya was seeing all this and tears were running down her face.

"This is exactly what happened to Anton," she said quietly as Ksenia came closer.

Ksenia nodded with a saddened look on her face and continued helping Lera to the car. Vadym and Olesya followed them. It was tragic seeing so many innocent people trying to get to safety and getting mindlessly killed. When they were all inside the car and positioned comfortably, Vadym started the engine of the car and drove off.

2nd of April
Mykolaiv

"All right then, Solomiya, the senior management has approved your request," Vira stated after seeking Solomiya out in one of the wards.

"Is this about Zlata?"

"Yes. I have some paperwork for you to sign. Here."

Solomiya took a sheet of paper from her and had a look. It was merely a confirmation that approval was granted and that Zlata would be in Solomiya's care and Solomiya would be solely responsible for the girl's wellbeing. Solomiya took out a pen and signed the sheet.

"Perfect. There's no better person to look after her," Vira said. "When we asked her if she wanted to come and live with you, she agreed right away. You two have bonded very closely. I'm impressed."

"That we have," Solomiya confirmed.

"Great. Well, she'll be discharged tomorrow. Her condition has been stable for several days and she is continuing to recover. I think that is in large part thanks to you," Vira praised her. "In other news, more wounded soldiers have just arrived. Can you help out in providing care for them?"

"Of course."

Vira mentioned in which ward the wounded were delivered and Solomiya proceeded. When Solomiya got there, she saw a lot of tattered and bloodied military clothes laying in a large pile in the corridor. It was apparent that some of the soldiers were wounded quite severely and their clothes needed to be removed completely and discarded.

When she entered one of the wards where the injured were brought, she saw three soldiers there, each one on a separate bed. One nurse was there already providing care. Solomiya approached the soldier laying at the very end of the room. He looked unconscious and was turned away, facing the wall. Solomiya came even closer and tried to turn him so that she could get a closer look at what happened to him. As soon as she touched him, he awoke and turned around sharply, looking all over the room in confusion. He was disoriented, but otherwise Solomiya could not see any major injuries.

"Where am I?" he asked in a mild sense of panic.

"You're in a hospital."

"What city?"

"Mykolaiv."

"Oh, thank God. I made it."

Solomiya noticed that he was wearing a Russian army uniform. He must've been another enemy soldier that was captured and needed treatment.

"You made it, but the rest of your unit are dead," Solomiya stated firmly.

"My unit? Oh, you're mistaken. I'm not one of the orcs."

"It doesn't matter. We provide medical care for everyone, regardless of whether they're Ukrainian, Russian or some other nationality."

"It does matter! I'm not a Russian soldier! My name is Roman Bilyk. I was stationed in Kherson. They took me as a prisoner when they took control of the city. For a whole month they beat and humiliated us until we broke out of there. Only about a dozen of us survived. Three of us headed here to speak with your commanders and send them a message."

"What message?"

"I can't give you the details. I need to speak to your commanders. All I can say is that things in Kherson will be changing. There will be a lot of partisan activity there in the weeks to come. We're hoping to collaborate with the forces here."

"All right. I'll inform them of your request, but you need to stay here as you're in no condition to be up and about yet."

"I know. One of us stepped on a landmine and died. I was thankfully not too close, but the shockwave from the explosion tossed me aside and I can't remember anything after that."

Solomiya inspected his arms carefully and noticed a handful of mild burns. They weren't serious, but it was a good idea to apply an ointment, which she began looking for in a nearby medicine cabinet. Roman suddenly remembered something and sat up.

"I need also to get in contact with someone. A new friend I made during my time in captivity wanted for his wife to know that he's alive and he asked me to relay that message. I intend to keep that promise as I know how important it is for loved ones to be informed of something such as this."

"Ok. Don't get out of bed. I'll go and get someone. They'll direct you to the right people," Solomiya said and decided to appease his requests as he seemed determined to get up and carry them out himself, which was not the best thing to do in his condition.

"Thank you," Roman showed his appreciation.

Solomiya hastily walked out of the room and decided that she needed to find Vira and relay Roman's requests to her. If this man was being truthful, then it was important that his requests were taken seriously as this would greatly help their forces in pushing the enemy back and eventually liberating Kherson.

2nd of April
Kherson

It was evening time and Taras finally reached his apartment building. It took a few days for him and the other surviving prisoners to sneak into Kherson and to remain inconspicuous so not to draw attention to themselves from the enemy soldiers who were now stationed in many places all over the city. The other survivors separated from him and he was now all alone, finally back home. After a month of captivity, he could finally be somewhere safe.

He went up several flights of stairs till he reached his apartment's front door. Of course he did not have his apartment keys anymore as all his personal possessions were taken during his captivity and he never saw a trace of most of them. However, he came prepared. On the way here he found a couple of wires that he could use as a lockpick. Serving in police for several years, lockpicking was something he learnt when tracking down criminals and locating them in their hiding spots.

He looked around to make sure there was nobody in the vicinity. He did not want the neighbours asking questions in case they saw something. When he confirmed that it was clear, he knelt down slightly, inserted the wires into the lock and began patiently picking the lock. When he heard a satisfactory click, he felt pleased that he had not gone rusty on this useful skill.

When inside his apartment, he locked the door, not wanting to be disturbed. The apartment was just as he left it. A warm feeling of comfort took over and surrounded him. For a whole month, he had to put up with filthy and cramped conditions and threats of being beaten and humiliated at any moment, waking or otherwise. For the first time in a long time he could relax.

Walking through the apartment, he began thinking of his family again, missing them, wishing he could at least speak to them for a few seconds and to hear their voices. He entered his and his wife's bedroom and gazed around, taking it all in as if afraid this place would get smitten from existence. As he approached the wardrobe, he couldn't help himself. He took out one of Vika's favourite dresses and smelled it. There were still mild traces of her perfume on it. He remembered her delicate touch and her compassionate voice, wishing she was near so that he could hug her.

He spent several minutes in the bedroom, looking through each item of her clothing and remembering when she wore each one of them. After that he walked into the room of both of his sons. Again he stood for a few moments and took the views of the room in, trying to make sure he would not ever forget it. He approached a desk by one of the walls and looked around the objects on it. A few of their books and toys were left behind, so he carefully looked at every single one of them, wishing he could spend more time playing with his sons and just having fun.

"When will I see you all again?" he asked himself, wondering if the answer would ever become certain.

He could've chosen to flee Kherson to another part of Ukraine and see his family there, but he knew that right now there were bigger matters at hand. Now he had to do everything in his power to save the city from occupation. The others who were imprisoned with him have gone to their own homes and families, but they agreed to meet once every week and decide on what to do. They would do everything possible to encourage fellow patriots and to terrify the enemy that was unwanted here. But they needed to be extremely careful and take precautions.

When Taras exited his sons' room, he walked up to a large mirror on a wall, seeing the rugged state he was now in. However, such look would be beneficial. A messy beard that grew out during this month and a bruised face from countless beatings he received would make him less recognizable to anyone who knew him, such as the others who worked in the police with him. He had no idea if any of them were collaborating with the enemy, so he needed to make sure they did not know of his presence in the city. The mission ahead would be extremely hard and could take months, but he was prepared to do everything possible for its success.

2nd of April
Kropyvnytskyi

Lera was in a hospital, getting treated for her injuries. She now had managed to shower and to change her clothes. Ksenia offered some of her own clothes to Lera and was there in the ward with her. A nurse who went by the name Nadiya was checking Lera and giving her the necessary treatment.

"There are no serious injuries thankfully," Nadiya said. "You might get occasional headaches in the next few days, but they will subside in time. I'll prescribe a medication for you to take when that happens."

"Thank you," Lera said in response.

"Hey, don't be so glum. You'll feel better soon."

"It's not that. I really miss my family. My brother stayed in Mariupol and was taken by the Russian forces. I worry for him. I don't know when I'll see him again. Maybe I never will!"

Nadiya didn't say anything and simply went silent. Her face got sadder. Ksenia was listening to everything too, and she also looked sad when Lera said this.

"You know, I cannot imagine what you're going through," Nadiya began after a few silent moments. "All I can say is that many good people lost their loved ones because of this cruel invasion. Many people had suffered greatly and lost everything. But we should never give up. A good friend of mine who lost the man she loved said this to me in the early days of the invasion – we're all going through our own personal battle against the darkness, and if we overcome this darkness, only then we'll prevail and move forward."

"This darkness has already consumed me," Lera stated sorrowfully.

"It seems that way, but you wouldn't be here if that was the case. You wouldn't be dreaming and hoping to see your brother. When the darkness consumes you, there's no more hope left."

Lera thought about those words and decided to take them on board. Perhaps the nurse was right. Keeping her hope alive might just help her get through this.

When Nadiya finished prescribing the medication and handed it over, Lera and Ksenia left the ward and began making their way through the corridors to exit the hospital. Lera continued pondering on what the nurse told her. She did not want to give up, even though she kept feeling like she should.

"You can stay with us for as long as you need," Ksenia said. "My parents' home has a couple of spare rooms. There should be enough space for all of us."

"Thanks. I don't know what to do with my life at the moment," Lera admitted whilst looking down at the floor. "I lost everything. I have no direction and no goal."

"For now your goal is simply to recover, physically and mentally. You've been through hell and need some time to yourself. Perhaps we'll take a walk through some nice places in Vinnytsia. I'll show you around the city. How does that sound?"

"That sounds wonderful. Really, thank you for everything."

They left the hospital building and headed for the car where Vadym and Olesya were waiting. The evening sky was already very dark. Lera stopped for a moment and gazed up at it, wondering if Danyil was looking at the same sky at that very moment.

"I hope you are still alive, my dear brother," she whispered quietly to herself. "No, I know you are still alive. I can feel it. I know you are strong, but I still hope you are not suffering. I can never forget all those times we were all together as a family, with our mum and dad being home. Those times will never happen again. They are gone forever. But I will never give up my dream that I will see you again someday. This is the only thing that will keep me going through this pain."

3rd of April
Near the Russian border

It was very early in the morning. Danyil was sitting at the back of a truck along with several other people, hands tied. He spent the last three days in solitary confinement and on some occasions received beatings by the sadistic Russian soldiers who wanted to teach him a lesson. And now he was being forcefully deported to Russia against his will.

What awaited him there was anybody's guess. He already knew that Russian soldiers were deporting ordinary Ukrainian civilians from occupied territories to the mainland Russia, and now he was one of the victims. If a Ukrainian citizen didn't show any defiance and was lucky, they would be sent somewhere more or less normal. If they were in the same situation he was in, then they were likely heading straight to a labour camp or to some remote part of Russia, such as freezing and isolated settlements in Siberia or the Sakhalin Island.

He looked out of the truck and saw several military checkpoints ahead. They were well-guarded with many armed soldiers crawling all over the place. He was genuinely scared. Mariupol during bombardment was hell, but at least it was a familiar place and he was not all alone. Now he was alone and was being taken someplace unfamiliar where he would be treated as less than a human.

He looked up at the sky, at the clouds, at the faint beams of sunlight, and he thought of Lera and wondered if she was safe at that very moment. He was thankful that he managed to get her out of Mariupol, but he had no clue where she was and if she was cared for and in safety. She could've been all alone, looking for food and shelter. She could've been hurt.

"Never give up, my dear sister," he muttered quietly whilst continuing to look up at the sky. "We'll reunite, I promise you. I'll do all I can to get out of this place. And once I do, I will find you."

3rd of April
Outskirts of Kyiv

Oleksiy was finally able to take a break from helping out and decided to visit Dmytro in the hospital, as well as to check up on Maria and Alina, who were in the same hospital. He got a chance to take a short walk with Max too, who missed him greatly and was delighted to see him. When they got to the hospital entrance, Oleksiy had to leave Max outside before going in.

He approached the reception desk to find out on which floor and ward his friend Dmytro was located. The receptionist had a look through the register carefully and informed Oleksiy of where to find his friend. Oleksiy then asked about Maria and Alina too. He was concerned for their wellbeing ever since that day that he found them in the woods.

When he knew where to go, he headed to one of the upper floors to check up on Dmytro first. On the way up the stairs his mother Irina phoned him.

"Yes, mum? How are you?"

"We're fine, dear. And you? Are you safe and healthy? You didn't get hurt, did you?"

"No, no, I'm ok, mum. Just came to a hospital to visit Dmytro. Remember I said that he got really hurt?"

"Yes, I remember. We heard the news that the enemy is retreating from Kyiv area. Diana and I were discussing of coming back home sometime soon, since it should be safer in Kyiv now."

Oleksiy felt a sense of elation coming up inside of him at the news that his mum and sister would be coming back and that he would see them once again. However, it was still dangerous in the country, as shelling continued happening all over Ukraine.

"This is great news, mum, but are you sure about that? It's still not safe, you know."

"I know, but we would like to be there for you and stick together as a family, just like we stuck together after we lost your father."

Oleksiy didn't argue. It was pleasant for him to hear that his family was coming back home and that the enemy was on the run. The tide was turning in their favour and life was returning back to some sense of normality.

He then spoke to his sister for a bit. She said she couldn't wait to return home and to see him again. At the end of the conversation, both Irina and Diana wished him to stay safe and for Dmytro to get better too, and then they ended the call. Oleksiy was now on the correct floor. He just needed to find the right ward.

After passing through a few identical-looking corridors, he found the room where his friend was kept. Dmytro was in a hospital bed, having his lunch, and Liliya was there with him. They were both pleased to see Oleksiy.

"Look who's finally come to visit me," Dmytro said jokingly. "I hope you didn't get yourself into too many sticky situations without me."

"It's been challenging, but also very eye-opening," Oleksiy admitted. "A lot has happened these past few days. The orcs are retreating."

"Not retreating. They're running away like cowards. I always knew our brethren would teach them a lesson."

"How has your health been? I know it's not been easy for you."

"Well, it sucks to lose half of your leg. My life will not be the same anymore. They said they'll attach a prosthetic there, so I'll at least be able to walk, but don't be expecting me to run any marathons in my life."

"We're lucky that the explosive did not kill you. I was really worried that you were gone at that moment when it exploded and threw you onto the ground."

"It will take more than that to kill me, brother," Dmytro always preferred to remain hopeful and trusted his own strength and luck.

"Well, you're not invincible," Liliya responded to him at that moment, "so please try to be more careful next time."

"I know. I'm sorry."

"And you too, Oleksiy. Keep yourself safe, all right?"

Oleksiy nodded to show his understanding of what Liliya said. Life was fragile, and one small mistake could leave a person a cripple for life or to rob them off their life entirely. After the recent days, seeing everything he had seen, Oleksiy understood the fragility of life more than ever before.

"Do you know when you're going to get discharged?" he then wondered.

"Not a clue. In two days they're planning to attach a prosthetic where my leg used to be. Once they do that, they'll have to watch me for a bit to make sure I'm ok."

Oleksiy then sat down and told Dmytro and Liliya about how the last few days had gone for him and what he was doing. They were listening to him with great intrigue. Dmytro regretted that he was not there, feeling like he was missing out. Half an hour flew by and then Oleksiy mentioned he'd be visiting him again and left the ward.

Maria and Alina were on the next floor up from what Oleksiy was told, so he made his way there and sought out the ward. He managed to find them without any problems. Maria was awake and was talking to her daughter. Alina smiled when she saw Oleksiy and greeted him.

"I just came to check how you've been recovering," he said to Maria.

"Getting better," she replied. "I had a lung infection and was getting very feverish."

"You've been through a lot, perhaps that's why."

"I wouldn't wish anyone to go through what we've seen in Bucha," Maria stated with a melancholy tone in her voice.

"I know. I've seen the aftermath of it all yesterday. I have no words to describe it. A part of me wishes I'd never seen that. I still can't believe that human beings could do something like this."

"They lost their humanity long ago, and during these days they tried to take ours away from us too. It's a consolation at least that they've been expelled from there and all the other surrounding areas. With each day they were there, they inflicted torment on people living there. They are demons, you understand! Human beings do not do such things to one another, especially brotherly nations."

"I agree with you. They will pay for all that they did. I am sure of it. We will never forgive them that."

"But I am thankful that I still have my daughter and that she is unharmed. Thank you, Oleksiy, for your help. We are both indebted to you."

"I am just glad I was there at the time and could help you."

"It was more than just help. You saved our lives."

Oleksiy was taken by such words. Until now, he never really saw it that way. But now, realising that he was the reason both Maria and Alina were safe and healthy, it gave him a sense of encouragement and inner strength. He felt that he was on the right path for the first time in his life, on a path to help people and to do the right thing. Maria grabbed his hand with both of hers.

"Thank you again," she said in a quiet voice. "Nowadays, I want to express my gratitude for everything good that happens to us and for all the good people that cross our paths. So I am thankful that whoever is watching us from above had brought you into our lives."

Oleksiy thanked her for the kind words and then promised that he would check up on them both again the next day and would help them find a place to stay once they left the hospital. He was determined to do everything he could to help them. He knew he didn't have the means to help the whole country, but if he could help at least someone, it meant a lot already and made a difference.

3ʳᵈ of April
Mykolaiv

Solomiya was returning home from her shift, and this time Zlata was with her. Zlata was finally discharged from the hospital and she was coming to live with Solomiya. Solomiya was glad that she managed to handle everything regarding paperwork so that Zlata could come and live with her, and Zlata was relieved to have someone kind like Solomiya in her life after she lost her parents. Solomiya knew that the girl missed her parents greatly and the thought of them was at the back of her mind, but she was determined to provide a sense of security and stability for the poor girl and to surround her with love at such a difficult time.

Solomiya was still a bit concerned as she knew it would be very difficult for her to both look after Zlata and to visit her work. She was given three days off to help Zlata adjust to a new place, but after that things would be challenging. On top of that, she wanted to arrange for Zlata to have an operation to get a prosthetic arm once things calmed down a bit, and this too wouldn't be easy. Despite that, she felt more determined than at any other time since the invasion began. She felt as though the fluctuations in her life were stabilizing and a clear direction was forming.

They both went up the stairs of the apartment building. Solomiya unlocked the front door and welcomed her new friend in. Zlata hesitantly entered and began looking around as soon as she walked in.

"What is it, Zlata? Everything ok?"

"Just had a strange feeling like I had to look around to see if it was safe. What happened to my home and my parents is still haunting me."

"I understand. But we'll do all we can and take as many precautions as necessary to keep this little sanctuary of ours safe. Sounds good?"

"Yes."

Solomiya helped her to take the coat off and brought her bags to a spare room. She already had time the previous two days to prepare the room for Zlata's arrival, so everything was in its place. She then returned back to the apartment lobby. Zlata was already in the living room, looking around.

"Do you feel hungry? Or perhaps you'd like a cup of tea?" Solomiya asked.

"A cup of tea would be great. But only if you're also going to have it."

"I will."

Zlata's eyes stopped on a photograph that was standing on one of the shelves of a cabinet. It was one of the photos of Solomiya together with Tymur. She picked up the photograph with great care and looked at it.

"Is this Tymur?" she asked.

"Yes," Solomiya confirmed and looked down at the ground. Remembering Tymur still brought a lot of pain to her heart. She kept questioning herself and wondering if she could've done something to save him, and each time she asked herself those questions, she never had clear answers.

"He's got a very handsome and kind face," Zlata commented. "I'm so sorry he is not here with us. You look so happy together on here."

"Yeah. I don't know if I'll ever fully recover from the pain of losing him. I really loved him, you know? It wasn't just a relationship. Life with him was everything I've ever dreamed of. His absence will forever leave a mark on my heart. I'm sure I'll learn to live with it, but that's all it will be – just coping and getting used to the pain."

Zlata put down the photograph on its original place and then walked up to Solomiya and gave her a big hug with her one good arm. Solomiya hugged her back. They both knew what it's like to lose someone dear and they both wanted to support one another, to face their pain together rather than alone. Solomiya did not know what the next few weeks or even months would bring and when the war would come to an end. But she knew that at least she was no longer alone to face the adversity. She had Zlata and Zlata had her, and getting through this cruel and horrifying war was now a little bit less painful.

Thank you for reading this book!

Credits and Thanks:

Font used for the book and chapter titles: Capture Smallz by Magique Fonts

Images on the cover designed in Daz3D Studio.

Assets used for the cover image are by the following artists:
The DigiVault, Stonemason, Dreamlight, Chungdan, Nikisatez, RedzStudio, Propschick, Sprite, PixelTizzyFit, Mousso, P3Design, ThreeDigital, Dogz, Zev0, Emrys, Fuseling, Sickleyield, Dark-Elf, CynderBlue